The Zombie Diaries

Books 1 to 8

Mark Mulle

PUBLISHED BY:

Mark Mulle

Copyright © 2015

TABLE OF CONTENTS

Book 1: Out of My Territory

Day 1

Braaaaaaaaaains.

Hah, got you there. Bet you thought I was going to eat you. Come on, don't be silly. I wouldn't do that. Not to you at least. You don't look like you've got much in terms of the brain department. Again, I'm kidding. Just a little joke. Hello there, I'm Romero!

So yeah, I'm what you might call a zombie. Which is extremely offensive by the way. We prefer the term 'undead brain munchers'. But, I suppose that's a bit too much to ask, so I guess we'll stick with zombie for the time being.

I live in a cave. It's cold, damp and dark, just the way I like it. I don't know if you're aware, but we zombies don't like the sun. In fact, we're allergic. Hah, I'm kidding. No, but seriously, we'll burn to death if we get caught in the sunlight.

Alright, all jokes aside, welcome to my diary. This is a record of my adventures throughout Minecraft. If you're my little sister, then put it down. If you aren't, then please keep reading. I hope you have a ghoulish time. Hehehehe.

Day 2

Sup creeps? Romero the zombie here.

Not much has happened. Not much ever happens around here. That's how I like it, though. I've never been one to 'run with the pack', or in this case, herd. A few years back, I moved out to the countryside. I found this excellent cave and I've been living here ever since. But enough about my life story.

Tomorrow, I'm going hunting. For some food. And no, I know what you're thinking. I'm not like a regular zombie who attacks other people. I'm what you might call a vegetarian. I already mentioned I'm not like other zombies. But we all have to eat something, right? The normal undead eat people and I eat salads. That stuff is delicious. Except for broccoli. One of these days I shall banish that vegetable to The Nether.

Anyways, that about does it for this entry. I'll see you all on the next one.

Day 3

What a tasty evening.

That's something we zombies say. If we go out to eat and if we enjoyed our meal, then we say 'what a tasty evening'. And it certainly was. I especially enjoyed chasing after a pair of humans for a few hundred blocks. No, I didn't eat them. We've been over this before. It was just for fun. And hey, it keeps me in shape.

Don't tell me you thought I went to a restaurant. Please, those places don't serve my kind. No shirt, no shoes, no life, no service.

Anyways, long story short, a couple of young, wannabe adventurers came onto my land and I ended up scaring them off. It wasn't even much of a challenge. They weren't even equipped with weapons, and the best they could throw at me was a stick. They actually threw a stick at me. I'm not one of those wolf creatures. What did they expect me to do, fetch it?

Well, looks like things aren't going to get any more exciting around here any time soon. Again, I love living in the peaceful countryside. It'd just be nice if a real challenge came along every once in a while. Maybe even an army of humans.

Day 4

Let's get one thing straight. I like my routine. I get up, have a bowl of mushroom stew, and lounge about in my cave till sunset. Then I go out and scare off all the humans who try to come near my cave, before going home and getting to bed before sunrise.

It's a nice routine and I enjoy it. What I don't like is a human ruining my garden.

Last night, some humans showed up. I was worried, thinking they were here to kill me. But they weren't zombie hunters or anything, just some builders.

Anyways, they cut down some trees and mined some stone from the cave entrance. I think they were scared of going inside. As they should have been!

Still, I was fine with them taking resources. People need to make a living – I get it.

Then they tore up my nice flowers.

The flowers I'd spent the past two hours gathering.

It took me nearly twenty minutes to find the red ones! And they just pulled them out of the ground.

I regret what I said about wanting a challenge. Still, I hope they realize that this means war.

Day 5

The war has begun.

The humans have begun building a house on what was once my garden. They appear to be using the resources they gathered. Resources I'll soon be taking back.

I got the chance to count them. Six humans. The good news is that they don't seem too heavily armed. Like I said before, they're builders. I think they're building some sort of tower. But this is no laughing matter. I'm a joker and I know how serious this is. If they get this tower built, it'll be a lot safer for humans to travel here. To me, safety and humans don't mix.

I need a plan to get rid of these builders. I considered attacking them, but it looks like one of them has a very pointy stick. Translation: sword. I'll need to find a way to get rid of him. Once he's out of the way, I should be able to force the rest of them off of my territory.

No one builds on my land and gets away with it.

Day 6

Too easy.

First things first: the humans are still here. They've cut down more trees and they've started coming into the cave. I was worried they'd find my house, but they didn't get too far.

And they won't get any further.

Last night, while most of them were sleeping in their campsite, one of them went for a walk. Alone. No weapons. It was certainly the perfect moment to chase one of them off.

Have you ever been walking along, minding your own business, when someone comes up behind you and grabs you, making you jump? Well, I had the same idea for this guy.

He was sitting by the lake in the moonlight, his back turned to me. I figured just a gentle tap and one look at my face would be enough to send him running. However, I might have overdone it a little.

I opened my mouth to utter the famous words "Boo", but I ended up growling instead. I swear, the guy jumped about five blocks into the air and fell into the lake. I had trouble containing my laughter as he swam off into the night.

Day 7

Maybe scaring that human away wasn't such a good idea.

This morning, I watched the group from behind a shaded tree. Let's just say they weren't exactly cheering when they found out one of their buddies was missing. Hey, I did them a favor. That's one less mouth to feed now.

Instead, they refused to appreciate my kindness and decided to set up a search party. Which just bites. They searched part of the forest and even one of the rivers near my cave, but they didn't find him. Of course they weren't going to find him. He probably ran all the way back to his mom's house.

So, what now? Well, I'm not sure. They don't look like they have a lot of experience fighting,

I'll have to think of a plan to get rid of the lot of them. For now, though, I'd best get some sleep.

Five humans to go.

Day 8

Okay. Things aren't looking good.

Those humans are still looking for their friend. Man, why can't they just forget about him? Why not get another human to replace him? Not that big of a deal, right? Apparently it is, because they're getting ready to search my cave.

From what I understood, one of them saw a zombie nearby. Figures. Before you ask, no, it wasn't me. I'm stealthy. I'm like an ocelot on a zipline. Heck, I once won an award for Most Stealthy Zombie.

No, they must have seen one of the slightly stupider zombies. Translation: A zombie with half a brain cell. Those things wander around and eat anything that isn't nailed to the floor. They also groan every five seconds, which you can hear about a hundred blocks away.

I'm not like them. I'm resourceful. I'm smart. I know what I'm doing. I can mine. I can craft.

Heh. Guess you can call me a 'Minecrafter'. Get it? No? Oh, come on, that was a good joke!

Day 9

Things are getting worse.

It's been about three days since I sent that human on his nighttime swim. All jokes aside, I watched the builders for most of the morning. They've stopped focusing on the tower, instead gathered supplies to make weapons. If I heard them correctly (I only got a B in English on my last test), then they'll be journeying into the cave tomorrow.

That gives me twenty-four Minecraft hours to think of something to stop them. And I believe I have an idea in mind. It'll take some work, but if all goes according to plan, it'll halt the humans dead in their tracks and send them running back to their villages, or wherever they live. And in case any of you are angry at me, let me remind you that they started it. They just had to trample my flowers.

My roses will be avenged, humans. You shall know the reckoning of Romero the Zombie!

They stopped working after I scared one of them off.

Day 10

It worked!

Okay, so those humans have been at it again. They spent the whole morning preparing everything they needed for the cave expedition. They fashioned a few makeshift swords and some torches. I wasn't too worried about them – only the guy with the iron sword. Those things sting. A LOT.

Anyways, I spent the morning cooking up a human recipe. No, I wasn't baking humans. I already told you I don't eat them. I was making 'smooth stone'. Basically what the walls of my cave look like before you mine it.

After I had a stack or so, I got to work on blocking the path to the entrance. I then placed some gravel on top of the barricade. If I was correct, the humans would attempt to mine through and instead find themselves buried. Ingenious!

As you probably guessed, it worked very well.

That night, I heard them digging through the walls.

A few seconds later, I heard them screaming. I got up and peeked through a crack in the wall. One of them had disappeared, his items floating around on the cave floor where he'd once stood.

Four humans to go.

Day 11

I thought those humans would have left by now. They've lost two of their group already. What reason do they have to stick around?

It looks like they have plenty of reason. Even with two builders missing, they're making work on the tower. Which is still on my land. I might have let it go if they'd bothered to move the darned thing, but no. Now that I think about it, if I let them finish, it'll be a real eye sore. If I ever want to move, how will I ever sell my cave with THAT sitting a few blocks away?

The problem is, however, that they know something isn't right. They've posted the guy with the iron sword by the cave entrance. I don't think they saw me, but they definitely know that there are zombies in the area. At the moment, I can't leave my cave. I knew I should have bought the emergency escape hatch extra when I paid for this place.

Guess that just means I'll have to make my own.

Day 12

Work on the Super-Secret Mega Ultra Escape Tunnel has begun.

At the moment, I can only work on it during the day, when the sound of building covers up the noise my pickaxe makes. I'm also not as strong as I used to be (all those Gummy Steves I've been eating). The years of living out here have made me weaker. Perhaps I should start doing some push-ups. Anyways, long story short, the exit is taking longer to dig than I'd like.

The humans are about 25% finished with the tower. The foundation has been completed and they've started smelting sand for glass. Pfft. These people have no taste in interior design. I'm telling you, those glass windows are going to look horrible. No Minecraftian has ever made a decent window. Have you seen them? They've got smudges all over them. Ridiculous, I tell you.

I'll finish the tunnel tomorrow.

Day 13

Yeah, about what I said yesterday. I don't think I'll be able to finish the tunnel today.

I've run into a couple of problems. The first is that my pickaxe has broken. I was trying to mine a really annoying piece of gold ore and my tool just snapped. This would be fine, if I had the materials to replace it. Unfortunately, I've used up a lot of my stuff trying to get rid of those humans.

The next problem is that the humans received a package today. Seeing as their weapons just weren't great, they ordered some from one of the cities. They're now equipped with bows and some arrows. Did I ever tell you about the time I took an arrow to the knee? It's a funny story. Of course, all my stories are funny.

I'll have to save my tale for another time. My foes now have bows, and if I overheard them correctly, one of them is going to visit the nearby village to pick up some armor. My only option is to attack tonight, while Mr. Iron Sword fetches the supplies.

I'd ask you to wish me luck, but I don't need it.

Day 14

Okay, maybe I did need it.

First things first, I'll tell you about the mission. My objective was to sneak into the enemy campsite, steal some of their supplies and, if possible, give them a good scare while I was there. I accomplished two of those goals.

Seeing as there wasn't any guard by the cave, I got out without a problem. I had the chance to look at the tower a little more closely. It looks as if the first floor is just about finished. They've installed windows, a door, and built some pretty tough walls. I'll have to find a way to destroy it at some point.

After I was done sightseeing, I approached the camp. They were all asleep, but had their weapons close by. I ignored them for the moment, instead opening a chest they'd left lying around. I filled my pockets with iron ingots and threw a couple of pickaxes on my back.

That's when they woke up.

I'm back at the cave now. They got me with an

arrow, though. I'll write some more tomorrow. I'm sure I'll feel better if I get some sleep.

Day 15

Yay, I'm still alive!

Of course I was going to make it, though. I'm Romero the Zombie. There isn't a human alive who can defeat me. (Except maybe that iron sword guy. I told you guys how much I hated iron, right?)

Anyways, when I was raiding their camp last night, I accidentally made a bit too much noise. One of the guards woke up and immediately shot me with his bow. Ouch. Thanks for that, guy. I'll be sure to send you a Christmas card this year.

I don't think they know that I'm a zombie. Much to my offense, they think I'm a rogue human who's stealing their stuff. How dare they! At least give me the credit I deserve. I'm the scariest zombie around, after all.

As if that weren't bad enough, Ol' Ironsword has returned. With the armor. Four sets of leather. This is extremely bad news. Now that they're a lot more dangerous, it's going to be a lot more difficult to get rid of them. I don't know why, but they seem to think they're braver when they're wearing that stuff.

Ah well, nothing can stop me from scaring them!

Day 16

Okay, apparently they do have something to stop me.

That's right. The cowards didn't even have the nerve to face me in battle, or at least rock paper scissors. While I was catching up on some much-needed sleep, the humans blocked off the opening to my cave with some strange black material. Whatever it is, my pickaxe can't mine through it. They have effectively trapped me in here.

Or they would have, were I not close to finishing the Super-Secret Mega Ultra Escape Tunnel. Those iron pickaxes are perfect for mining through stone. I would be finished by now, but mining has been a bit painful recently, considering my injuries. My best bet would probably be to make my way out of here. As long as I can sneak in and out of my cave, I think I can get the upper hand here.

I haven't had the best week. But don't worry; I'm sure I'll feel better tomorrow.

Yeah, this isn't funny.

Day 17

I do not feel better.

No, in fact, I think I'm even angrier.

So the good news is that the Super-Secret Mega Ultra Escape Tunnel is now complete. The exit comes out behind what was once a lovely hill. A hill that I used to climb up on to watch the stars. After escaping from my underground prison, however, I discovered that this hill no longer exists. Why? Because those stinking humans dug it up!

How on earth do you dig an entire hill up? That's what I'm wondering. Apparently, they needed the dirt to reconstruct the land around the tower. I'm still wondering what they did with the spare dirt blocks. Maybe they had a snowball fight? But instead of snowballs, they used dirtballs. Heh. Gotta write that one down.

Anyways, they've certainly made progress on the tower. It's two stories high now. Once they complete the roof, it'll be finished. And somehow, I don't think the humans will be pleased with what's happened here. I have a feeling this place will be full of Minecraft soldiers soon.

Well, unless I have something to say about it.

Day 18

So, I think I have a plan to defeat the humans.

Right now, they think the rogue human (zombie) is trapped in the cave with no way out. Excellent. I hope they keep thinking that. They won't be as careful now. Anyways, there's no way I can face them. Not now that they have weapons and armor. Although it pains me to say it, I don't think I'll be scaring them the normal way.

But that doesn't mean I'm going to leave them alone.

If my plan works, then I won't need to scare them. You see, when I was looking through their chest the other night, I found something I'd never seen before. I've heard humans talk about this magical device, but I didn't think it existed.

An object with the ability to create fire.

I wonder how they made it. Maybe they found it somewhere? Doesn't matter. When I was out exploring, I noticed that their tower is made almost entirely of wood.

Only the floors are made of stone.

I think we're all scared of a little fire, don't you?

Day 19

Hello there, good sir, welcome to our restaurant.

I'm Romero, and I'll be your waiter this evening. Please, allow me to start you off with some of that broccoli stuff you seem to enjoy so much. You may wash that down with a glass of our finest Weakness Potion (a delicacy among my kind). Once you've finished with that, might I provide you with some entertainment? Tonight's show involves some wonderful frights!

This restaurant sounds like somewhere I'd like to eat. I think I'll move to somewhere with a place like that once I've dealt with these humans. I doubt this area is going to look nice after that tower has burnt down.

Alright then, looks like the sun is going down. Time to put the plan into action. Just this once, I'll let you wish me luck.

May the blocks be with me. Haha. I'm on fire. Well, I'm not. But they will be.

Day 20

Oh man, the looks on their faces.

Haha. Hahaha.

I snuck out through the Super-Secret Mega Ultra Escape Tunnel. Man, that name is catchy. As if things could get any better, they've all started sleeping in the tower. Not even a guard to keep watch. Of course, they thought I was stuck in the cave. Silly humans.

I had another peek in their chest. It was mostly empty. I'm guessing they moved most of their stuff inside. I did, however, find some torches. Just what I needed. I lit them, then tossed them through the window.

It didn't take long for the place to catch fire.

Although I may have overdone it a bit, once they woke up and saw the place was on fire, they ran for the hills. I had to stifle my laughter as I saw Ol' Ironsword flee from the tower, his pants burning. I gave him a wave as he ran off into the distance.

Looks like Romero wins again. There isn't a human alive who can defeat me.

Day 21

Okay, I might have gotten it wrong when I said there weren't any humans left.

There are now twenty humans. Not just builders. Soldiers.

You remember that guy I pushed off the ledge? Yeah, well, it turns out he didn't exactly run home to his mom's house. In fact, he just happened to run into some fisherman by the lake, who took him to the nearby village.

Anyways, that particular human spent a few days in the village, before heading back to the building site. He turned up last night, after I'd burnt the tower to the ground. Within a few hours, he'd bought a horse from the village and travelled to one of the much bigger towns. There, he was able to get some of their soldiers to come with him.

As I normally do, I listened in on the humans from behind my shady tree. These warriors are apparently looking for a 'griefer', which I believe is human speak for a 'really bad human'. Again, I'm really offended. I'm a zombie, for crying out loud!

Still, looks like I need a new plan.

Day 22

Just when you thought things were bad, they get even worse!

Heard that line in a movie once. It was about two humans, unfortunately. Why can't they ever have zombies as the main characters? Anyways, enough of my rambling.

I took the time to spy on the soldiers today. Looks like they're much better equipped than the builders. Chainmail armor and iron swords seem to be the norm. Gah, how I detest iron. It is perhaps the most evil of building materials. One day, I shall seek out all iron and destroy it!

Oh great, I'm rambling again. The point is that these soldiers are pretty tough looking. I'll have to use my big brain if I'm going to get rid of them. I know what you're thinking, and yes, zombies do have big brains. Most of them just don't know how to use them. Not me, however. Not Romero the zombie.

I'm kind of big-headed at times, aren't I?

Still, as long as they don't find the Super-Secret Mega Ultra Escape Tunnel, I'll be fine.

Day 23

They've found it!

The Super-Secret Mega Ultra Escape Tunnel! They were able to find it! Oh, how could this have happened? That thing was practically camouflaged. I must have placed at least two leaf blocks on top of it!

You're probably wondering how I know they found it. Well, it goes a little something like this. One of the soldiers stumbled upon it and decided to journey into the cave. At the time, I was busy making some mushroom soup, so you could imagine my surprise when I heard him clatter into my cave. The armor he wore was hardly the best for sneaking around. He should take some ninja lessons from me.

Anyways, I was able to slip away and crouch behind some nearby rocks. Unfortunately, he found my little workstation. The workbench, the stove, the chests, and yes, even the mushroom soup. That human actually had the nerve to eat my food. Get your own food, man! Doesn't he know mushroom soup is a personal favorite of fine?

But yes, they've found the entrance. Time is running out.

Seriously, how did they find this?

Day 24

Alright, Operation Save My Flesh is a go!

I listened in on the warriors again. Looks like they believe that the 'griefer' is hiding within the cave and is using the Super-Secret Mega Ultra Escape Tunnel to come and go without attracting attention. Well done, Sherlock, but you got one detail wrong. I'm not a griefer! I'm a zombie! This type of behavior is normal for our kind.

There is no way I can take on all these humans. I considered hiding within the deeper parts of the cave, but while this place is a maze, I'd have to eat at some point. Besides, there's no guarantee they wouldn't find me. No, I need to find a way to dispose of all of them.

I was looking through the supplies I stole through the humans, and I found something that might help. I have no idea what they were planning to do with this, nor do I know how a bucket can hold something this hot, but it might just be what saves me.

Last I checked, humans aren't lava-proof.

Day 25

Humans certainly aren't lava proof, but they are pretty darn quick.

Last night was going to be the moment to strike. They're still getting ready to assault the cave. I nearly had a heart attack when I left via the Super-Secret Mega Ultra Escape Tunnel, as they had someone on guard. Luckily for me, he was too busy picking his nose. Still, it was pretty gross.

I positioned myself on what used to be my favorite hill. It overlooked their camp perfectly. With the bucket of lava in hand, I was planning on tipping it out and watching it flood their little base before they even realized what was happening.

I failed to account for how slow lava is.

That stuff took about ten minutes to reach the base of their camp, and by that time, the humans were all awake. Half had their weapons drawn and the other half were throwing water everywhere. What's worse, that place lit up the area like a Christmas tree. I'm pretty sure they saw who I was.

I think I preferred 'griefer'. I do not like being called a 'human in a zombie mask'.

Day 26

I was incredibly lucky last night.

I had to sprint my way out of there (zombies don't sprint, keep in mind), racing back into the Super-Secret Mega Ultra Escape Tunnel and blocking the path behind me. Last I heard, they're still trying to mine their way in here.

I don't have a lot of options left. Scratch that, I don't have any options left. Here I am, Romero, the funniest, most resourceful zombie in Minecraft, trapped in his cave by a bunch of humans. I don't have enough time to dig another escape route and hiding won't save me for long. That leaves me with only one choice.

I have to fight.

I've got a stone sword, a single leather cap, and a couple of arrows, but no bow. Heh, it's not like I need anything else anyway. I'm Romero the zombie! I truly am the funniest and most resourceful zombie in Minecraft. A bunch of humans with sharp sticks aren't going to defeat me.

Bring it on, I say! Bring it on!

Day 27

Yeah, no.

Maybe hiding in the caves for the rest of my days isn't such a bad idea. Maybe I can live off the mushrooms or something. Besides, it's not like the humans will look for me forever, right? They'll surely give up eventually.

Oh, who am I kidding? I couldn't fight them. I'm scared. I blocked off the tunnel with the last of my blocks, but that will buy me a few days at the most. But what else am I supposed to do? If I fight them, they'll cut me to pieces. If I hide, they'll catch me and throw me in prison.

Maybe I'll throw my diary at them. Who says words will never hurt you? Hahaha. That's a fantastic final joke. Even with everything that's happened, I'm still pretty funny. Guess I won't be moving away after all. Ah well, it's been a nice life. I've scared my fair share of humans. Guess I should have guessed they'd catch me eventually.

Nice knowing you. Thanks for reading this far. To whomever you are, never forget the legend of Romero, the greatest zombie who ever lived…

Day 28

There's still hope!

Last night, as I listened to the soldiers pound away with their pickaxes, I had a stroke of brilliance. I ran over to my chest, the chest containing all those stolen goods. I rummaged through them, looking for the red blocks. The ones I'd found at the very bottom of the chest. I'd seen them earlier, but completely forgotten about them.

I remember watching a documentary on TV once. It was about creepers, showing us what they were made of and what was inside of them. The exact same type of red block.

TNT.

The most destructive device in all of Minecraft. The true weapon of a Griefer. Perhaps my last chance at scaring away these soldiers. I need to get to work placing this stuff around the cave. Thank you, dear reader, for sticking with me. And no matter what happens, let me tell you…

It's going to be an explosive finale.

Yup. I still got it.

Day 29

This very morning, the soldiers finally broke through.

They were armed to the teeth, as one might say. Chainmail armor, enchanted bows, and those cursed iron swords. I never did tell you why I hated iron so much, did I? Another story for another day.

Twenty of them poured into the cave. I stood at the far side, watching them come in. It didn't take long for them to spot me, holding a redstone torch. They shouted orders, getting into position. Swords were readied, arrows were notched.

Haha. Notched.

I raised my hand, as if I was about to surrender. They all looked at one another. Had they never seen a zombie surrender before? Well, they'd never seen a zombie like me before. And this would be the last time they saw me.

It was then that they started to look a little closer. They noticed the red powder sprinkled on the floor, twisting and turning throughout the cave. Most of them didn't care, but a few of them followed it to its source.

Twelve blocks of TNT, positioned all around the cave.

I waved.

I dropped the torch.

Day 30

What a fun, crazy adventure this has been.

Dear reader, thank you for sticking by these past thirty days. It brings me great joy, knowing there is someone out there who is reading the great tale of Romero the zombie. I bet you're wondering what's happened since my last entry. Well, I'm glad you asked.

After I dropped the redstone torch, the explosion threw all of the soldiers backwards. It also blew up half of the cave. Whoops. Looks like I was going to have to move, even after all of that. I gathered up what few supplies I had left and got moving before the soldiers could get back up.

This has been one of the craziest adventures of my life. Even crazier than that one day I raced go-karts with a creeper. How those things drive, I have no idea. Still, I can't deny it's been fun. Who knows where the road is going to take me now?

This has been Romero, the craftiest, funniest, and most resourceful zombie there is. As to where I end up, dear reader, I hope you stick around to find out.

Good luck, and happy Minecrafting!

Book 2: To the City of Overwatch

Day 1

Coming soon to a theater near you, the must-see action film of the year. Featuring explosions, slow-motion and everyone's favorite Zombie...

Romero!

Hello there, dear reader. Back for another adventure? I can't say I blame you. Who wouldn't want to read about my exploits?

What's that? I'm being obnoxious? How dare you! I

don't care if it's true, I should just... Alright, fine.

Sorry about that, I was just talking to my new pal Dave. He's what you might call a slime. I found him shortly after I began my travels and we've been together ever since. It certainly was helpful that I'm fluent in Slimespeak. Along with fifty two and half other languages.

What was that? I'm bragging too much again? You little pest, I'm going to squish you Dave!

Aside from picking up an annoying little creature for my journey, things have been pretty quiet. Just the way I like it, as you might remember. I've been travelling on the world, looking for a place to take my talents. Ignore what the slime is saying; my talents are highly sought after.

I warn you now dear reader, I doubt things will be as calm as they were last time. For the faint hearted, this diary won't be for you. Wherever Romero goes, adventure and danger are bound to follow.

Stick around. You won't regret it.

Day 2

Dear Diary,

Romero here again. I'm still on the road and danger is coming from all directions.

Do you remember my last adventure? About how I defended my land from some builders and then an army of soldiers? Yes Dave, it was an entire army. Anyways, if you don't recall, I had to stun the soldiers with some TNT to escape them. I thought it would be years before they'd have the chance to catch up with me. Turns out I was slightly off with my estimate. It's only taken them a week to pick up on my trail.

To be honest, I was lucky. I was just about to bathe in the local river when I heard the hooves of horses and the yelling of several people. I immediately dived into the lake, hiding beneath the water as the soldiers emerged from one of the forest paths.

Thankfully, Zombies don't have to breathe. I could stay down here as long as I wanted, without any consequences. I didn't dare peak my head out of the water to listen in on their conversation. Instead I waited, growing tense as one of the horses started drinking from the lake. Eventually, they all dispersed in different directions.

As far as I know, they're still tracking me. I'm not entirely sure how I'm going to get rid of them, but I know where I'm heading. The nearby Minecraftian city of Overwatch. If all goes well, I'll never be chased by humans again.

Day 3

I think I have a plan.

Dave and I spent the night hiding in a tree. Not exactly my first choice. Personally, I would have preferred my cozy bed back at my cave. Can't really sleep there though, considering I blew the place up. Perhaps I should have thought that plan over a bit more. It didn't really occur to me at the time that detonating a dozen or so blocks of TNT in your home was a bad idea.

Those warriors must have been searching for half the evening, but they didn't spot us. Not even when I started throwing apples at them. Haha, silly humans. Still, I need a way to escape them. I can't spend the rest of my life hiding in trees, my only source of fun coming from throwing fruit and talking to the Jell-o cube.

Yes Dave? What do you mean that's offensive? I should be more considerate towards other mobs? Y'know, I've had just about enough of you. Ow! Okay, fine. He just bit me. The little pest. Back to my master plan though. Humans like to chase Zombies. Zombies like to chase humans. But have you ever seen humans chasing other humans?

I'm smart enough to pass for a human. I just need to find a way to look like one.

Day 4

Stealth mission, begin.

While the humans slept, I gathered the supplies necessary to my success. Seeing as I couldn't head into town resembling a creature from a horror movie, I needed to fashion a disguise. Luckily for me, I knew just the place to shop for my materials.

As Dave kept watch, I snuck into the soldiers' camp. They were still fairly beat up after our last encounter, and hadn't bothered to post a guard. What a shame, that made things way too easy. The first thing on my list was armor. I searched through a couple of their backpacks, looking for something ideal. The warriors were all equipped with chainmail, though I wasn't too interested in that. It makes way too much noise when you're moving and weighs an absolute ton. Plus, I think they'd notice if their top notch equipment went missing.

Instead, I found an old leather chestplate and leggings. I doubt they'd miss them and besides, they go so well with my hat. All I need is a nice pair of booties and I've got a complete outfit. Oh yeah, I also made sure to 'borrow' a few Emeralds. One or two from each soldier, just so they wouldn't pick up on their missing money. To complete my outfit, I poached a cape and hood. This would keep my face and hands hidden. Apparently most humans don't have green skin, so it might look a bit out of place.

For now however, I say goodbye.

To my readers, up until this point, you have known me as Romero the Zombie. It is here that I must abandon my identity. From now on, call me Romero the human. Blergh. It doesn't have a nice ring to it at all.

Day 5

I am now one with the humans.

Greetings diary. I bring good news. Dave and I have successfully infiltrated the city of Overwatch. It's not a bad place once you get used to the lack of open spaces and other monsters. Sure, I can't stand other Zombies, but it was nice to know they were around. This place feels empty, even with the hundreds of people roaming the streets.

I was worried about getting in at first. The only way in is through the main gate, carefully guarded by some of the fiercest looking soldiers I've ever seen. Covered head-to-toe in iron armor, never taking their gaze off of people who dared to enter. One of them even had a pair of diamond swords!

Despite the menacing guards, I was able to enter the city without any trouble. One particular warrior gave me a sideways glance, but throwing an emerald in his direction distracted him somewhat. The city itself wasn't much to behold. A collection of wood and stone houses, all mushed together. The lack of creativity is appalling.

I'm currently staying in 'Creeper's Rest', the cheapest inn I could find. I paid the man a few emeralds and rented a room with a balcony. I didn't stick around to speak to the other guests. True, I know the human language, though I have somewhat of a gravely accent. They'd think something was up if I talked to them for an extended period of time.

I'll explore the city tomorrow. For now, I need to get some rest.

Day 6

I must say, I was somewhat impressed by this place.

I went to explore the city today. Dave complained about have a sore bottom from hopping around too much (the lazy cube sits on my shoulder most of the time), so I went to explore on my own.

Overwatch is one of the many human cities. It's composed of two sections: The Outer Layer and The Inner Layer. The Outer Layer is the place where all the people live. It has many houses, shops, inns and even a theatre. The Inner Layer is where the bulk of the soldiers reside. It's protected by a second wall and an even tougher gate than the entrance. There, you'll find the keep and Overwatch's renowned prison. Access is restricted unless you're a soldier or have good reason to be there.

I visited a few of the stores. I wasn't too bothered about the Blacksmith or the Farmer's Market, though I did quite enjoy the apothecary. You know, the kind of place where they make potions. I ended up purchasing a couple of Weakness Potions. Hey, I did once tell you they're a delicacy among my kind!

I also took the time to browse Craft Co. I ended up buying a few supplies to tinker around with (some gunpowder, a few pieces of string, a few planks of wood and a fishing rod). I've probably spent a bit more than I should have. I've only got twenty emeralds left. I'll soon look at getting a job to restore my finances.

The supplies I bought. I'll have to think of a use for them.

I'm quite enjoying myself at the moment, but I mustn't let my guard down. After all, I have a mission to complete.

Day 7

It occurs to me that you might not know why I've come to Overwatch.

Admittedly, it wasn't just for safety and a means of escaping the soldiers. I do in fact have a very good reason for infiltrating this city and attempting to gain the trust of the humans.

During my brief adventuring experience, I stopped by a local inn. Seeing as I had no disguise at the time, my plan was to burst through the door and frighten everyone away. Afterwards, I'd take as many bowls of mushroom stew as I could fit in my pockets, before fleeing to the hills.

A sound plan. It would have worked too. However, as I was about to burst through the door, waving my hands and yelling "Boo!" I heard the humans speaking. Muttering at first, before it evolved into loud cheering.

"Another bowl for Captain Rick, the Bane of Zombies!"

Captain Rick. A well-known Zombie Hunter. He

captures my species and has them work in XP Grinders. There's history between me and him, but more on that later.

Listening in on their conversation, I overheard some startling facts. Captain Rick and his men have captured a few dozen Zombies, dragging them off to Overwatch for some unknown reason. They must have been fairly stupid for Rick to catch them. Still, I'm not going to leave them at the mercy of that Zombie Hunter.

This is my mission. Free the Zombies, take over the town and scare Captain Rick into retirement.

This town will soon belong to the undead.

Day 8

Operation 'As Yet Untitled' is now underway.

Yeah, I still need to think of a cool name. Dave thinks I should call it Operation 'Romero gets his butt handed to Captain Rick', though I'm not really sure I like it. Silly names aside, I've started planning out the rescue mission. At the moment, there are three main goals:

- Infiltrate the prison.

- Release the Zombies.

- Scare 'Captain Rick' and his men away from Overwatch.

If I can complete those three tasks, then the mission will be a success. Of course, this won't be easy. Not by a long shot. In fact, if it were anyone else, I don't think they could do it. Still, I'm not just anyone. I'm Romero the Zombie! The smartest, the craftiest and of course, the funniest.

Dave, this isn't the time for your snide remarks. I have things to plan. Why don't you go play with your ball or something? Sorry about that. Anyways for everything to go smoothly, I'm going to need to obtain some specific items. I think I can craft some of the things I'll need. However, to ensure maximum success, I'm going to need a guard uniform. I'm also going to need the keys to the cells.

So far, things are going well. And as a plus, it doesn't look like they'll be changing any time soon.

Day 9

I think people are starting to get suspicious of me.

This evening, I went down to the dining area for a bowl of Mushroom Soup. I did my usual routine, pointing to the meal I wanted and paying the amount in full. Up until now, the inn keeper never said anything about my silence, only served my food with a smile and a nod. Notice how I said up until now.

"So mister, mind me asking why you don't like to talk?

Curses. He just had to be the curious type.

"Sore throat," I shrugged, "I can't seem to get over it."

At the time, I thought that was an excellent cover story. For about five seconds.

"I've got a spare Potion of Healing in the back room. A few swigs of that and you'll be feeling right as rain."

"Oh, I wouldn't want to be a bother," I shook my head.

"It's no trouble. It's only been gathering dust back there."

Why do you people have to act so generous?

"I assure you, I'm fine," I protested, "Never liked the taste of those things anyway."

The inn keeper looked at me for a few more seconds, before sighing and occupying himself by cleaning a glass. As I took my Mushroom Soup, I noticed a few of the patrons were giving me odd looks. I quickly excused myself and returned to my room. I tried telling Dave what had happened, but he snoozed off halfway through my story.

I have to be more careful. If the humans found out there's a Zombie living among them, who knows what they'll do?

Day 10

I checked out The Inner Layer today.

I didn't get the chance to go inside. Only soldiers are authorized, which is why I'll need the uniform. Instead, I pretended to be a citizen walking around the streets. I kept my hood up and leather cap on, afraid the watchmen on the walls might spot me. Thankfully, they seemed more interested in their food than what I was up to.

Dave sat on my shoulder the whole time, making remarks about how he was bored and wanted to do something entertaining. I'm starting to regret ever picking this little guy up. He doesn't really do that much, except eat, sleep, complain and criticize me. I'm certainly not obnoxious. Just because I'm better than most people doesn't mean he has to be jealous.

My rambling aside, I confirmed that the only way into The Inner Layer is through the gate. I think my best bet of sneaking in would be hiding in a group of them. I've seen them question individual soldiers, but never entire scouting parties.

As I headed back to the inn, I almost ran into that man with diamond swords. He ignored me, brushing past in a brutish manner. While he was calm, I felt dizzy. I set off in the opposite direction, back to the inn as fast as I could.

It's not every day you pass Captain Rick on the streets.

Day 11

I spent the day inside today.

After my fateful encounter with that maniac, I feared for my life. Well, fear is the wrong word. Romero is never scared. I was just concerned. I'd passed within a few blocks of the guy, yet he'd paid me no heed. I spent the night wondering whether or not he'd turn up at the inn with a battalion of soldiers to drag me off to Overwatch's prison.

Looks like my fe- I mean, concerns, were misplaced. Captain Rick obviously didn't recognize me, thank Notch. My disguise is certainly working. I think for now, I'll avoid going near The Inner Layer until it's time for the operation. There's no new information to gain from staring at the walls for hours on end.

I think my best bet will be to remain at the inn for a while. There's not a doubt in my mind that some people here know more than they should. If I overhear a juicy bit of gossip, or perhaps listen to some off-duty guards, I might pick up on something that will give me an edge.

I won't be beaten. I'll find a way to rescue my

fellow species and to give Captain Rick the greatest fright of his life.

Day 12

Dear diary, I bring good news.

No Dave, we're not shopping for new hats. I'm fabulous enough without one. Apologies once again about my companion. Still, we're not here to talk about him. You're here to read about how my day went. Well dear reader, I shall tell you!

As I said before, I've stuck to the inn. Staying away from public life has turned out to be an effective strategy. Listening to the conversations of numerous people has given me several useful facts. For one, I now know that the butcher sells bat meat. I'm still vegetarian, but if I wasn't, I'd certainly avoid that particular store.

What truly interested me however was the amount of guards who came in here. They'd munch up their Mushroom Soup or whatever it was the innkeeper was serving, before discussing this or moaning about that. Already I know that there's a shortage of arrows and that a few of the warriors have lost their jobs. It appears this place isn't as well guarded as I first thought. But that's not the best bit.

I overheard that the soldiers are going fishing tomorrow. I don't think there will be a better time to 'borrow' one of their uniforms. It's what I'll need if I want my plan to succeed.

Day 13

Who doesn't love fishing?

I can say without a doubt that I hate it. Catching those poor, defenseless animals? Despicable. I'm a vegetarian, don't you know? Why do you think I have such a love for Mushroom Soup and Salad? Still, it gave me all the more reason to go through with the mission.

There were five guards with the day off. As it so happens, there's a lake that resides within the city walls, connecting to one of the rivers. It's where the humans would be going fishing. It's also where I would be going fishing, though not for food.

I followed them from a distance, sticking to the trees that lined the path. When they eventually picked a spot, I began the patient process of waiting for the correct moment to strike. It didn't take long. They threw their backpacks off to one side and started tossing their rods into the lake. With a light step and an even lighter touch, I crept from my hiding place and unzipped one of the bags.

"Hey Jim, can you get the bait from my backpack?"

If I had a heart, it probably would have stopped at that very moment. There was no way I could hide fast enough. All they had to do was turn their heads. They were going to catch me!

"Paul you simpleton, you're sitting on them!"

Heh, suckers. After I was finished looting, I fled back to town before they could come up with any more excuses to go through their stuff. I doubt a misplaced uniform will go unnoticed, but I doubt I'll need to be here much longer. If all goes to plan, I'll have the prisoners rescued in a few days.

Day 14

As I feared, the soldiers have begun a search.

A missing uniform was obviously going to turn a few heads, and now a couple of the guards have been asking around, asking if people have any information. Overwatch is fairly crime free, so it's not often a theft is committed. And it's not like I stole a piece of bread from a shop. This is a soldier's uniform I've got stashed under my bed. If they find it, there's going to be massive trouble.

I kept myself to myself, sitting in the corner and sipping at my drink as they questioned the innkeeper. Thankfully, they didn't ask around the inn. There must have been three-dozen people there, and I don't think they fancied spending half the day here. They left fairly quickly, taking my nervousness with them.

Not that I was nervous in any way of course. Romero is never nervous about anything. I am truly and utterly without fear. Be quiet Dave, you were too scared to read 'My Little Skeleton'.

On a lighter note, I have a name for the mission.

Operation Undead Breakout.

Day 15

Reader, the day is nearly here.

The guards sure do have big mouths. I overheard them barking about an expedition team which will be returning tomorrow. That will serve as the perfect cover to enter The Inner Layer. Once inside, I'll find a way to obtain the key to the jail cell. As soon as I have that, it will be a simple matter of scaring off the guards and freeing the Zombies.

Of course, I make it sound easy. And as skilled as I may be, I understand that I shall be faced with certain danger. Therefore, if I do not return from this mission, I leave everything to Dave the Slime. He's sticking behind to guard the room (as he so claims) and won't be accompanying me into The Inner Layer. As he's the only friend I really have, I have no choice but to give him everything I own if I don't make it back.

Hah, jokes on him, he'll be stuck with the rent.

Everything is ready. Tomorrow I'll break my fellow Zombies free and teach Captain Rick a lesson he won't soon forget.

Day 16

Well, that could have gone better.

Ladies and gentlemen, I regret to inform you that Operation Undead Breakout has failed.

Things had been going perfectly. The expedition team returned right on time, heading straight for The Inner Layer. I'd been crouched behind one of the houses, waiting for them to show up. They hadn't bothered to arrange themselves in a marching formation or anything, so it was easy to slip into the group. Good thing the uniform fitted me correctly.

As I suspected before, the guards didn't bother checking the entire group. They just nodded to the captain and opened the gates a few seconds later. This was it. At long last, I had access to The Inner Layer. The men in front of me were beginning to enter. Just a few more moments and I'd been inside…

"GRIEFERS!" I heard one of the soldiers yell.

I turned. Sure enough, a group of nasty looking

fighters were racing towards the open gate. They weren't messing around, armed with some dangerous looking blades and firing arrows at the guards. You guys remember that I was dressed in a uniform at that moment in time, right?

I immediately ran off into the alleyways, ignoring shouts from the other soldiers about me being a 'coward'. If they wanted to get into a fight, it was none of my business. I certainly wasn't going to stick my hide on the line for them. Of course, it only occurred to me after I'd removed the uniform and replaced it with my leather armor that I missed my opportunity to reach the prison.

I'll just have to think of something else. Still, that's what I'm best at.

Day 17

Romero here.

Things aren't looking great. The guards have been on high-alert since those 'griefers' decided to attack The Inner Layer. Who those people were or why they decided to do it, I'll never know. They did however; mess up my chances of getting inside. The soldiers are checking everyone who goes inside now, and they've been pressing the townspeople for information.

Time is running out. If I can't find a way to free the Zombies within a few days, I'll have no choice but to flee the city. I can't sit around, waiting for someone to see through my disguise. I've already heard that Captain Rick himself is leading the search for the griefers.

I'm forming the basis of a new plan to infiltrate The Inner Layer. The original plan had me entering and leaving without anyone suspecting who I was. My new idea will get me inside, but my identity will be revealed if I'm caught. Therefore, I must be extremely careful to avoid detection.

I'll stay at the inn until I'm ready to move out. I'll just have to keep myself occupied by playing cards with Dave. Pretty sure he cheats at it.

Day 18

I never told you the history between Captain Rick and myself, did I?

I suppose now is a good a time as any. The fact is, this isn't the first time I've encountered the diamond-sword wielding warrior. In fact, he and I once fought perhaps the greatest battle of my young life.

It was a few years ago. Captain Rick (who'd been a mere Zombie Hunter back then) had heard rumors of a Zombie who enjoyed scaring people, but refused to eat them. That Zombie was me of course. Of course, young Rick got it in his head that he would capture me and put an end to all the fright.

At the time, I lived in a swamp. I'd been lying in wait for my next victim, not expecting him to be the very bane of my existence. Rick entered my lands and began searching for me, calling out to me and naming me a coward.

I too was much younger, and much more foolish. I dived out of my hiding place, letting loose the most threatening roar I could muster. I figured Rick would flee in the opposite direction, but instead he spun round and sliced me with an Iron Sword.

I barely escaped that day. I fled the swamp, sold it for next to nothing and moved into my old cave. You've probably guessed where I got my fear from iron now. All because Captain Rick decided to come and hunt me down. Well, I'm hunting him now and things are going to go a little different this time.

Day 19

Time truly is running out.

Rick and his men visited the inn today, demanding to know about the griefers. The moment I saw him approaching through the window, I fled to my room. I made a quick escape by jumping off the balcony and spent the day exploring the town. I didn't dare return back until later that night.

When I made it back, the innkeeper was complaining that Captain Rick had driven away most of his patrons. I'm not surprised. That man truly is aggressive and barbaric. The only way to defeat such a man is through a calm mind and a bit of creative thinking.

Fortunately, I have both.

I've been working on a solution to my various problems. With The Inner Layer so heavily defended, gaining access will be a tough challenge. Even without the guards, I'm still faced with a massive gate that bars entrance to those deemed unworthy. Still, being the ever-crafty zombie that I am, I have come up with the ultimate solution.

If this works, then those gates won't be a problem anymore.

Day 20

I'm finished.

This is perhaps my greatest invention yet. Truly, I will go down in history as one of Minecraft's greatest inventors. Everywhere, people will scream my name from the rooftops. Heck, I'll probably be given a national holiday I'm that clever.

Yes Dave, I'm being big headed. I agree. But I think I deserve it this time. I truly have come up with an amazing item. It's a shame no one else will get to enjoy it. Ah well. Maybe when I'm done here I'll retire and mass-produce the things. Zombies everywhere will have the power to go where they wish.

Right, I should probably explain the item. It's what you might call a ''grappling hook'. I assembled it out of hooks from fishing rods, pieces of string and a few planks of wood. The supplies I gathered when I first came to this city.

Seeing as I can no longer enter through The Inner Layer's main gate, I have taken it upon myself to find another way in. With this device, I can ascend the walls and make my way to the prison.

Oh yes, that reminds me. I don't think I'll be needing the key to the cells anymore. Not with my second greatest invention…

Day 21

This is my final day in Overwatch.

Tomorrow, I'll execute that prison break if it's the last thing I ever do. Those Zombies have waited long enough. For all I know, Captain Rick has his XP Grinder set up already. I'm not about to leave them to such a fate.

I spent the day enjoying myself. I went for a walk around town, ate a few bowls of mushroom soup, bought a dozen Weakness Potions and even treated myself to a cookie with my last few emeralds. I certainly won't be needing them after this.

You know, these humans aren't all that bad. Sure they'd probably freak out if they knew who (or what) I truly was, but that doesn't matter. I think I've misjudged most of them. All of my life, I've spent scaring these poor creatures away from my land. Sure, a few of them deserved it (those builders and the soldiers especially), but I think I have a newfound respect for them. They're just trying to live their life. Just like me.

I'm off to bed. I've got a big day tomorrow and I

need to be energized for it. And besides, even if I might not dislike humans as much as I once did, there's still one in particular who deserves what's coming to him…

Day 22

I left the inn late that night, having spent most of the day in my room.

The streets were eerily quiet, lacking the hustle and bustle you found in the busy morning. Just the way I liked it. Passing the locked stores and darkened houses, I soon found myself standing outside of The Inner Layer. My eyes glanced over the walls, spotting a few guards with their torches looking thoroughly bored.

Luckily for them, things were about to get exciting.

First of all, I removed the miniature explosive from my pocket. My second greatest invention. TNT was useful, but it was too darned heavy to carry around everywhere. I lit the fuse with my trust Flint and Steel, before tossing the small cube into the gate.

It immediately exploded, throwing back the giant wooden door with an almighty bang. That certainly caught the attention of the soldiers. Some peered over the walls, looking for the attacker, while others raced to defend the gate. Exactly as planned.

With their focus distracted, I pulled out the grappling gun and, begging to Notch it would work, fired it. The hooks buried themselves within the cobblestone walls and stayed there. With a grin, I began reeling myself in. I ascended upwards, pulling myself onto the walls. At long last, I was in The Inner Layer. As much as I wanted to admire the view however, I had work to do.

Leaving the guards to investigate 'The Mystery of the Exploding Gate', I carefully maneuvered myself across the battlements. I kept to the shadows, try to avoid drawing any attention to myself, before reaching the entrance to the prison cells.

I found it unguarded. So far, so good. The prison was built to house thousands, cramming hundreds of Zombies into each and every cell. It was sickening. At any rate, they didn't seem to notice I'd arrived.

"Attention fellow Zombies, your savior is here!" I cried out. A few turned their heads, but they remained unimpressed. Time to shake things up.

"Stand back," I warned, throwing the explosives at the iron doors. A loud boom filled the air, followed by a metallic clang as the door fell off its hinges. The Zombies looked at one another, obviously confused. I sighed. They never had been too bright.

"You are free," I told them, "Go and scare some humans or something."

That was my first objective accomplished. With the hundreds of undead I'd just released, I doubted the guards would stick around to fight. They'd be forced to flee the city. I felt a pang of guilt, thinking of all the innocent humans who weren't involved in this. Still, it was necessary. The zombies came before the humans.

"YOU, STOP!"

I turned. Captain Rick and two of his men were standing by the prison entrance, weapons drawn. The regular Zombies sensed an easy meal, while I sensed the possibility to escape. I gave Rick a mocking bow, before tearing off through the opposite door. I heard him yell fruitlessly behind me, as hordes of the undead lurched after him.

I was greeted with a staircase leading to one of the upper towers. Excellent. Everything was still on track. Seeing as the Zombies had dealt with Captain Rick for me, all I had to do was escape The Inner Layer and I was home and dry. I passed by a few of the guards, though I paid them no attention. All that was left was to reach the top of the tower and take the staircase leading into the keep. After which, I'd head outside and use my grappling gun on the wall again. It was foolproof.

The warriors were gaining ground now. I had to hurry. The staircase came to an end, and I found myself at the highest point of the fortress. Below, I could see the burning gates. Behind me, I could see my enemies. Before me, I could see my escape. I gave my opponents a cheery farewell, before moving to turn the handle…

It was locked.

No, that couldn't be right. This wasn't according to the plan.

My escape route had been sealed from the other side, leaving me trapped on the castle roof, face to face with a dozen angry soldiers.

No escape.

Book 3: Terror Unleashed

Day 1

Well, this is a fine mess I've gotten myself into.

Oh, hello reader. Didn't expect to see me again, did you? I bet you thought I was finished. Surrounded by hundreds, no, thousands of soldiers, with no escape route in sight. Yes, from a normal perspective, it would seem that bad. But for I, the great and mighty Romero, there is truly nothing that I cannot accomplish.

Of course, you're probably wondering how I ended up in this prison cell. Well, I'll tell you. It's all part of the plan. The second stage of the operation if you like. Seeing as things went a bit south last time I wrote, I've been planning my next move to overthrow the humans and –

Oh who am I kidding? I got captured. The zombies were able to escape but I was trapped on one of the towers. I don't know how, but they'd somehow guessed I would take that route out of the castle. They sealed the door leading to the keep and left me trapped there.

Still, that doesn't matter at the moment. I failed, true. It happens to the best of us. It's not a problem. I'll soon find my way out of here and this wretched city. Once I do….

Dear reader, please stick around. The last two adventures were nothing compared with what's about to happen here. In fact, I daresay that it will be too exciting for most of you.

One thing is for certain. Romero still has a few tricks left up his sleeve.

Day 2

Stone-cold mushroom soup with stale bread. Yuck.

At least they remembered I'm a vegetarian. I gulped it down without saying a word, though I gave the jailer a look that would make an Enderman cringe. I'm the only intelligent zombie on this planet and this is how they treat me? Despicable, I say.

I haven't a clue what's going on in the outside world. I've only heard a few rumors from the guards, and they don't tend to talk much around me. Apparently any information they leak to me is dangerous. What do you expect me to do? Write a newspaper from my jail cell? Bravo guys, really.

I've been worried. Not so much about what will happen to me. When the time comes, I'll bust out of here. No, I've been worrying about Dave. Did the guards capture him too? Are they holding him in a cell here? He's a pain in my rear, but he's like family, even though I've known him for less than a month.

I'll write as soon as I've got something to report on.

For now, I'm going to see if I can dig through my Bedrock cell with a spoon.

Day 3

I suppose you're wondering how I'm actually writing this. After all, aren't I in jail?

Well yes, you're right about that. However, the guards were oh-so nice enough to let me have my diary. They also gave me a blunt pencil to write with. Yes, they're aware I'm intelligent. At least, the people at the prison are. From what I've seen, the soldiers are pretty worried. A Zombie who can think and speak? Their worst nightmare comes true.

When I'm bored, I'll often growl at them from behind the cell door. I kind of feel bad when they run off screaming for their mothers, but I've got to do something to occupy my time. Besides, scaring humans is kind of my thing.

Update! The Commander himself is coming to visit me tomorrow. Excellent. If I can subdue him, I might be able to sneak off in his uniform. Freedom is within sight!

Day 4

I've made a horrible mistake.

I have well and truly screwed up this time, even I
have to admit it. I should never have come to Overwatch. I
should never have tried to rescue the Zombies. I shouldn't
have even tried to get rid of Captain Rick.

It turns out there was a good reason for making an
XP Grinder.

Do you remember those Griefers who attacked The
Inner Layer? Turns out that isn't the first time they've tried
this. From what the Commander told me during his visit to
my cell, those Griefers have been wanting to take control of
the city for some time now. The guards protecting this
place are pretty tough, but it seems they're growing in
power. Up until last week however, it was a manageable
threat.

They've been up to no good during my stay in this
cell. More specifically, they've been gathering materials.
With most of the soldiers trying to contain the Zombie

outbreak, The Inner Layer was left weakened. The Griefers used this opportunity to break in and cause trouble.

The Commander was worried that they'd try to blow up some of the buildings. Strangely enough, the only place they attacked was The Vault, a place I didn't even know existed. Located under the prison, it houses some of the rarest and most powerful artefacts in Minecraft.

To cut a long story short, The Griefers stole something from The Vault. A set of keys known as The Eyes of Ender. Said to contain the power to unlock the door to a place known as The End. I'm sure I don't need to tell you that a place with a name like this is bad news.

Right, I forgot, the XP Grinder. It's a type of training machine. The Commander had those Zombies captured so that the soldiers could train with their weapons. He assured me that the Zombies had never been in any danger, and that he'd had no intention of harming them in the first place. In fact, they were even being fed!

And of course, I went and released them into Overwatch, which is currently infested with the undead.

Whoops...

Day 5

What an interesting day this turned out to be.

Romero here. They brought Dave to visit me. It sure was nice to see the little guy, even if he is a pain. He acted non-existence to my presence, but I had a feeling he'd missed me just as much as I missed him. At least the soldiers weren't going to punish him. I honestly wasn't expecting to see the little guy for a while.

Of course, I also wasn't expecting Captain Rick to come to my cell either.

At first, I was shocked. I thought the Zombies had gotten to him. Yet here he was, alive and well. And as much as I wanted to be angry at him, I couldn't find it in myself to hate him. He'd had good reason for taking my kind, in a way. Sure, I didn't like the fact they were being used for the humans to grow more powerful, but it wasn't like there were any other choice.

Everyone else had to leave when he arrived. He took a seat

"Romero."

"Rick."

"How's the scratch I gave you?"

"Healed up nicely. Haven't liked Iron since."

"Heh, I guess not."

"So, you're a Captain now?"

"Sure am. Maybe even a General someday."

"I wish you luck with that."

"Thanks."

What followed was a somewhat awkward silence. Here we were, two men (well, a man and a zombie) who'd once despised each other.

"Listen, Romero…"

I did, although I felt the urge to tell a joke. It was a good one too. Why did Steve cross the road? Anyone? Alright, I'll save it for later.

"This is going to sound crazy, but I think we're going to need your help."

He was right. About the crazy bit and the needing my help part.

Day 6

I met with Rick and the Commander today.

There was a lot of talking involved, let me tell you. I'm pretty sure I dozed off a few times. Something about evil, one part about a danger that was going to destroy the world, no more cookies for the children if these things happened. I only caught the gist of it.

"That's why we need you, Romero," the Commander finally said.

Wait, what?

"You're not like the other Zombies. We all know this. Heck, if you were a human you'd be considered a true genius. You breaking into The Inner Layer without any help is a great example of what you can achieve. I know our species have our differences and I know that things are tense right now, but we need to set aside our hatred for one another. If those Griefers open the gateway to The End, there's no telling what will happen."

As much as I didn't want to admit it, the human was

right. Sure they threw me in here (for a somewhat good reason), but there was no point in us fighting if there wasn't a world to fight over. I gave the two soldiers the best smile I could muster and extended my hand.

"It looks like we have work to do."

Day 7

Operation 'The Beginning' has begun.

Yes, I know, that is some of my worst material ever. But you have to admit, it's clever. At least Dave isn't around to insult my sense of humor. Besides, a couple of the guards snickered when I told them that one. Even Captain Rick had a smile on his face, and he's Captain Rick!

"Alright men," the Commander had summoned us all to the barracks, "As you may or may not know, we are enlisting the help of a Zombie. He's somewhat different to the ones you've encountered in this past. Everyone, meet Romero!"

"It's a pleasure to meet you all," I bowed.

At that precise moment, everyone started screaming.

"IT TALKS!" one of them cried before rushing to the nearest exit (which, unfortunately for him, was a window).

"SETTLE DOWN!" The Commander roared.

And so they did. Except the guy who jumped out the window. Pretty sure he won't be doing much for a while.

"Romero is going to help us defeat The Griefers and help recover Overwatch," Captain Rick explained.

I must have misheard him.

"What was that bit about recovering Overwatch?" I asked.

"Nothing major," The Commander explained, "We just need you to evict your zombie pals."

Well crud.

Day 8

First task, complete!

With The Outer Layer filled to the brim with Zombies, it was up to me to lead them off. Like a shepherd ordering about a flock of sheep I suppose.

I wasn't exactly happy with the state of the city. The townsfolk had locked themselves inside as soon as the zombies had reached The Outer Layer. The streets were filthy, the windows hadn't been cleaned and it stank something awful. They were spread out among the city, though the majority was located near The Inn.

"Alright you disgusting piles of flesh, this way!" I demanded, pointing towards the gate.

I must admit, they were a little reluctant to follow me. Instead, they were more intent on getting inside the locked-up buildings. They probably wanted some of that delicious Weakness Potion I enjoyed so very much. I can't blame them. At any rate, I needed to draw their attention away somehow. Seeing as they were looking for something to eat, I decided to offer them a top-notch (haha) meal.

"Attention Zombies, we have food!" I yelled (or rather, growled) to the horde, tossing a few bowls of mushroom soup outside the open gate.

Like metal to a magnet, the undead dashed towards their dinner. The message must have spread quickly among my kind, as soon the Zombies were outside the city and scrambling to grab a bowl.

"Wait a minute," I heard one of them moan, "This isn't meat. I don't even know what it is."

"It's the vegetarian option," I grinned, "NOW!"

The soldiers within the gatehouse pulled a lever, bringing the gate crashing back down. The Zombies pounded on the doorway, though it was a futile effort. They weren't getting back out any time soon.

Step one complete. Now on to Step two.

Day 9

With Overwatch (almost) Zombie free, it was time to plan a counterattack.

The Commander summoned me, Captain Rick and a dozen of the best soldiers in the city to his room. Dave also tagged along, hanging out on my shoulder like he normally does.

"Men -" he began, "- and zombie. We are gathered here today because Minecraft faces imminent danger. The likes of which we have not faced in years. The Griefers who have been bent on destroying our city have stolen one of our most dangerous artefacts. The Eyes of Ender."

It was as if the temperature in the room had dropped, even though the fire was blazing. The supposedly elite soldiers were now shaking and whimpering. I'm pretty sure one even cried out for his mother.

"Settle down," said the Commander, though even he looked a little pale, "They haven't done anything with them yet. In fact, the men I stationed at The Stronghold have told me everything is good. However, that doesn't mean they aren't preparing. No doubt they're getting ready to attack any day now."

"Our mission is to protect The Stronghold at all costs. We'll be heading over there in a few days to start building the defenses. When The Griefers do attack, we'll be waiting for them. We'll defeat them and retrieve The Eyes of Ender."

A murmur of approval sounded throughout the room.

"However," The Commander added, "we have to prepare for the worst. If The Griefers are successful in their mission, then Overwatch must stay standing. That's why I've sent message to every major city in Minecraft. Should the gateway be opened, this world could very well be destroyed."

I don't want the world to be destroyed. Most of my stuff is here.

Day 10

I've never seen the city so alive.

Since The Commander said that there was a possibility The Griefers could win, Overwatch has bustled with activity. The soldiers have been setting up defenses on the walls, the blacksmiths have been forging weapons and even the innkeeper has used this opportunity to sell his food.

So what now? Well, I'm just enjoying what time I have left here. The Commander said we won't be moving out for a few days, so I've spent many hours eating mushroom soup and drinking Weakness Potions. Captain Rick was kind enough to inform everyone in Overwatch that there was an intelligent Zombie roaming the streets, though that didn't make them any less wary of me. I tend to sit in a faraway corner, for their benefit of course. How lucky they are that I'm not like other Zombies.

For now, I guess I'll just spend my time at the inn. Maybe play some card games with Dave. Not much else to do around here, unfortunately. They wouldn't even let me in at the archery range. Apparently I'd frighten the kids. Of course I would, I was placed on this earth to scare people!

Ah, whatever. I'll just catch a few Zs. I'm not needed for a few days, right?

Day 11

Emergency.

The Commander received word from The Stronghold. Apparently, The Griefers are gathering outside and are preparing to siege the place.

Everyone is running around here like a Creeper without its head. Captain Rick's gathering his top soldiers, The Commander is barking orders and I'm sitting here munching on a cookie. Oh, now the Captain is giving me a look that could break Bedrock. Jeez, cut me a break. I scrubbed your city clean of Zombies and this is the thanks I get? Fine.

Still, maybe I should be a bit more serious. From what I know of The End and the general tone of people around here, it seems Minecraft might be in a little bit of danger. I say a little, when I really mean a massive amount of danger. So massive, they have not yet invented a word to describe it. I shall now invent said word. Gigantihumongous.

Looks like we're getting ready to move. It'll take us

all night to reach The Stronghold. If we don't leave now, we might not make it in time.

I've only heard rumors of what lurks in The End. Notch only knows what would happen if such a creature was released into this world.

Day 12

No.

We arrived early in the morning, our weapons at the ready. The entrance to The Stronghold was located in a massive cave system. Definitely the kind of place I'd want to live in when this was all over. Talk of my dream house aside, The Commander and Captain Rick led me and the other soldiers into the darkness, with only a simple torch to light our way.

Immediately, things were looking bad. A few of the Stronghold's guards were strewn across the floor, obviously knocked out. A short while later, we came across the entrance. An iron door had once protected it, though something had ripped it off its hinges. Just how strong were these people?

"We need to hurry," said Captain Rick, plunging into the tunnel ahead. The rest of us struggled to keep up with him.

Despite the danger, I took the time to admire the structure we were in. An ancient building from thousands of years ago is really interesting to look at. The bricks were some sort of unique stone. The rooms were decorated with fountains, bookshelves and on one occasion, a jail cell. Yet the closer we got to our destination, the more injured guards we found. Had they actually managed to take out a single Griefer?

"You don't know what you're doing!" Captain Rick barked from ahead. I picked up the pace, turning right into the final room.

"Oh I think we do," came the smooth reply.

It was eight against two. The Griefers had certainly upgraded their equipment since the last time we met. Iron armor, iron swords, iron underwear, iron everything! The cowards must have figured out my one weakness!

"I wouldn't worry too much Romero," Captain Rick grinned and spun his twin diamond blades, "That cheap tin won't stand up to our own equipment."

I took a moment to check my weapon, relived to see the gleam of a Gold sword. Not only was it fancy looking, but it would cut their armor to shreds.

"I'm afraid that won't matter Captain," the Griefer (who I guessed was their leader) was making his way to an object hovering at the center of the room. It appeared to be an inactive portal of some sorts. The blocks forming the structure each contained an Eye of Ender. Except for one. The last one.

"So what if you defeat us? It'll be too late after

that."

"I'm asking you not to do this," Rick sounded like he was genuinely troubled.

The rest of the soldiers had arrived by now. The Commander had a bow at the ready, his arrow trained on the object in the leader's hand.

"Listen here Griefer," he spoke, "drop the Eye of Ender and surrender. We've got you outnumbered!"

The Griefer didn't seem to care. He just laughed. Even his comrades looked a little concerned. Maybe they hadn't realized what coming here would mean and being captured by the Minecraftian Army.

"This is for all my companions you locked away!"

The leader inserted the final Eye of Ender, as The Commander fired his bow.

A brilliant flash of light illuminated the room, blinding those who were present. This was followed by a deafening roar. Great, we couldn't hear and we couldn't see. I ended up losing my footing and collapsing to the floor, grasping for the wall. Faintly, there was what sounded like the flapping of wings and the crumbling of bricks.

"This place is collapsing!"

"RUN!"

As everything went dark, I felt something grab

ahold of me…

When I woke, we were outside of the cave. Well, what had once been the cave. The entrance had collapsed, buried under a mountain of rock. We'd all escaped, but there was no sign of The Griefers.

"It's no good, we failed," I heard Captain Rick sigh, as another roar filled my eyes.

I turned my head just in time to watch a dragon fly into the clouds.

The creature the legends spoke of…

Day 13

I now know what The Griefers were trying to accomplish.

The Eyes of Ender. A set of keys required to open a portal to The End. This, I already knew. When I was younger, I remember my parents telling me stories of The Ancient Evil, said to be a powerful beast which lurked within this realm, trapped by Notch himself.

That beast, known as The Ender Dragon, is now free.

Already there have been reports of attacks on various villages. Whatever it is, it seems intent on destroying everything the humans have created. The soldiers are just as puzzled as I on how to combat it. All the warriors sent to defend the settlements have been unable to harm the creature. It's said to be invincible!

What now you might ask? How will humanity escape this predicament? They won't. At least, not without my help. Romero the Zombie, most intelligent among his kind and funniest creature this side of Minecraft. If there's anyone who can defeat The Ender Dragon, it is I!

You see, we might have found something. When Rick and I had run off to fight the Griefers, The Commander had discovered some sort of strange item in one of the chests. At first I thought it was iron, which nearly resulted in me fleeing to the hills. Because y'know, it obviously wasn't tough enough for me to face. Like I'd ever be scared of some iron.

Upon closer inspection however, the metal was much too dark to be iron. It reminded me of the material that was once used to block my cave entrance. Obsidian, I believe it's called.

Captain Rick said it himself. This could very well be what we need to defeat The Ender Dragon.

Day 14

Okay, good news and bad news.

The good news is that we can indeed forge a weapon from the material we found. The blacksmith isn't sure how however, considering every tool he's used on it has broken. Some of the soldiers are going to the villages to look for the proper tools. I'm going with them. Commander's orders, apparently. Seems like we need the equipment used by the villagers, said to hold some sort of magical properties.

The bad news however, is that The Ender Dragon is getting more and more violent. It's not just going after the smaller villages now. One of the larger towns, Craftville, is now in ruins. Almost no one knows how. Apparently the dragon crashed through every building in its path and set fire to the rest. Five years of work, now gone.

If something isn't done soon, The Ender Dragon will most likely attack Overwatch. Captain Rick mentioned the only reason he hasn't is because it's still building strength. Still? It's destroying settlements left and right.

This thing is more destructive than a hundred overcharged Creepers. How in the heck can it get any more powerful?

On a lighter note, it seems I'm indebted to the good Captain. I overheard one of the soldiers mention that Rick was the one who dragged me out of the Stronghold while it was collapsing. My once worst enemy has become a friend. Or at the very least, an ally. I'm not entirely sure what to think of this.

I'll write more tomorrow. For now, I'd better get ready for my trip tomorrow.

Day 15

I'm back at Overwatch.

Hello reader. You might be wondering why the visit to the village took less than a day. Well, it was planned to take much longer, until we received word that The Ender Dragon got there before we did.

That village is only two-thousand or so blocks away from Overwatch. Once a bustling little outpost, now a smoldering ruin. No one was hurt, but the villagers have had to flee here. Over two-hundred of them. The Commander isn't sure where they're all going to stay.

This is really bad news. If the blacksmith can't get his tools, how the heck can we forge a weapon to fight this thing? Captain Rick has talked with some of the villagers who are specialized in enchanting items, but I don't think it will be enough. And if Overwatch falls, who will be left to protect these lands?

It's funny, isn't it? Not the haha funny. The weird funny. About a month ago, I would have wanted this city torn to the ground. Instead, I find myself feeling scared and worried for the humans, villagers and other races of this world. This Ender Dragon isn't after anyone in particular. It just wants to destroy everything. To tear away all the creativity and imagination of this world.

I can't let that happen. It's my fault. The Ender Dragon has been released, and it's up to me to send him back to The End.

Day 16

Alright, there may be some hope after all.

Captain Rick has been speaking with a few of the refuges. Apparently, they used to gather resources for their tools from a secret mine. It was kept hidden so that no one else would use it, but with the threat of the dragon looming, they've given us the location. It's located north of Jeb's River. On horseback, we could probably reach it within a few hours.

Rick wants me to go with him. For some reason, he trusts me. Even after our history. To be honest, I'm happy to go with him. He's an excellent fighter and one of the few people who could probably take on that overgrown lizard.

We're leaving in a few minutes. Rick doesn't want to waste any time here. If The Ender Dragon reaches the mine before us, then we've lost. We need the resources there to make the weapon.

This might be my very last entry. If I don't make it back, then I leave half of my possessions to Dave the Slime and the other half to the people of the Overwatch. It's the least they deserve after all the trouble I've brought them.

Day 17

Hey diary.

Rick and I found the mine. Exactly where the villagers said it would be. Notch, bless those big-nosed freaks. The good captain had me stand guard at the entrance while he descended into the caverns. The villagers had told us there was a chest full of the tools we needed. If that was the case, we could have the blade fashioned by tomorrow.

My back against the mine entrance, I kept an eye out for potential danger. Surely no mob would dare to challenge the great Romero? Huh, I haven't said those words in a while. Even Dave doesn't remark on me being obnoxious anymore. Maybe I've changed. Still, any monsters who came over here would get a good walloping.

Those were my thoughts, until The Ender Dragon showed up.

I dived into a patch of grass, watching the beast hover over the mine. This was the first time I'd seen it up close. A dark, handsome creature with piercing purple eyes.

Its wings were stained black and grey. A trail of scales ran from its neck down to its blocky tail. Truly a fearsome monster.

Still, as long as nothing caught its attention, I was certain I would be –

"Hey Romero, I got the tools!" yelled Rick, emerging from the mine.

Yeah, humans are still pretty annoying.

We fled on horseback at maximum speed, The Ender Dragon breathing a few fireballs in our direction. Yet for some reason he didn't seem too interested in chasing us. I knew it. Too scared to fight the incredible Romero? Haha, I knew it. He took his rage out on the mine, flooding it with purple fire.

"Let's hope these tools work," I joked to Rick, who had to stifle his laughter.

Tomorrow, we forge the ultimate weapon.

Day 18

This was it.

We brought the Obsidian material and the tools to the blacksmith. He took them from us with a stern look.

"I hope you know what you're doing," he muttered, before starting his work. He had a point. If our plan didn't work, then nothing else would.

He worked all through the morning and long into the night. The other soldiers came and went, but Captain Rick and I stayed for the whole process, helping him with his work. We passed him the tools he needed, kept the furnace burning and, on one occasion, fed him dinner.

When he'd finished the initial blade, he plunged it into a cauldron of water. Thick steam filled the room as he brought the soon-to-be sword over to an anvil. He hammered down on the metal once, twice, a dozen or so times. When he was satisfied he set it to one side, before starting work on the hilt.

By the time the moon towered above the clouds, he

had finished.

Just from looking at it, I knew what kind of weapon we were wielding. An Eye of Ender was fitted into the pommel of the sword, staring at me with an empty gaze. The cross guard and handle were a beautiful silver coloring. But the blade... It was pure black, radiating waves of energy. Already, I knew of its power. It was stronger and more powerful than a thousand diamond blades.

But would it be enough to defeat The Ender Dragon?

Day 19

Romero doesn't feel fear, though he is a bit nervous right now.

There has been word from Block City, the second largest settlement in this area. The Ender Dragon has attacked, and despite the warriors putting up a brave fight, the city is no more. There are no other targets in the area. Tomorrow, The Ender Dragon will strike at Overwatch. If we fail to defeat it, then there will be nothing else standing in its way. It will travel across Minecraft, destroying everything in its path.

Captain Rick and The Commander have made all the preparations possible. The citizens have been evacuated for protection, while the army is staying behind to fight. The walls have been equipped with TNT cannons, and swords and arrows have been freshly sharpened.

Everyone is tense. They've never battled an enemy on this scale before. It will truly be the ultimate showdown.

Here's hoping we make it through tomorrow. I've still got many more stories to tell.

Day 20

The wait was the worst part.

Three hundred of us lined the walls. Myself, Captain Rick, The Commander and the soldiers. All of us united to defeat Minecraftia's greatest threat. An oversized lizard. Truly, this was the stuff of legends. Many years from now, they would remember us as the heroes who defended this world when no one else could.

It started raining, soaking my diary. I really wished that stupid beast would show up already.

Night had fallen by the time The Ender Dragon had arrived.

Like most guests would, it announced its arrival with a shriek that blew the eardrums of everyone present. Then, like a lance cutting through the air, it descended from the skies and towards the city.

"ARCHERS, FIRE!" bellowed The Commander.

On cue, fifty arrows took to the heavens, attempting to remove The Ender Dragon from its throne. It just snorted, letting off a quick stream of flames that roasted the projectiles.

"TNT CANNONS, TAKE HIM DOWN!"

The explosive flew next, two-dozen blocks of TNT looking to light up the sky like a fireworks show. I stood beside Captain Rick, watching the battle unfold before me. Maybe we wouldn't need the sword after all...

"Just how the heck can it do that?" demanded Rick.

The dragon twisted and curled its body, the bombs sailing past into the night sky. As the cannons prepared to reload, The Ender Dragon swooped down and crashed into them. The soldiers ducked, as our airborne opponent barely missed our heads. What it didn't miss were the TNT Cannons. I shuddered as the blocks themselves disappeared as it flew through them.

"This thing defies the laws of physics?" the color had drained from my companion's face.

"If it flies through the walls, there won't be anything left to protect the city," The Commander thought out loud.

As if it had heard, The Ender Dragon flew up high, too high for the archers to hit it. Upon reaching maximum altitude, it catapulted back down with speed that would shame an Olympic sprinter.

"DARN IT ROMERO, USE THE SWORD!"

I nodded, the creature growing closer with every

passing second. It was now or never. I pointed the blade at The Ender Dragon, the hilt suddenly growing hotter in my hand. My weapon began to shake and I struggled to hold onto it. The beast opened its maw to give us a fiery bath, just as a beam of white light shot out of the blade of my sword and down the dragon's throat.

"By Notch's beard, it works!" The Commander exclaimed as the soldiers cheered. The Ender Dragon writhed about in obvious pain. I guess that wasn't the kind of meal it wanted. Heh, I've still got it. Even in the face of danger, Romero is pretty dang funny.

"If the sword works, it'll create a portal to send the dragon back to its cursed dimension," I recalled the words of the blacksmith, "That's why I fitted an Eye of Ender into the hilt. Even a sword this powerful won't be enough. You have to send it back to its world." The Ender Dragon was stunned, though for how much longer I wasn't certain. This would be our only chance to defeat it.

The archers pelted it with arrows, as I twirled the blade and slammed it into the wall. The Eye of Ender began to glow, shooting off a surge of sparks. Just a few blocks away, a dark cloud of smoke began to form. It grew in size, transforming into a powerful vortex with the suction power of a hungry hippo. A portal back to The End.

It was drawing The Ender Dragon in, pulling the wounded beast to its prison once more. Even the soldiers were having trouble holding onto the wall. Weapons and armor were ripped into the tear into the sky, with our destructive foe drawing closer by the second.

"IT'S WORKING!" I yelled out, sticking my tongue out at the creature, "May Herobrine curse the rest of your days!"

I really should have thought twice about insulting it.

Using its claws, it gripped on to the sides of the portal. Desperately trying to remain within our dimension, it opened its mouth one final time. I understood perfectly. If it was going down, it was taking all of us with it.

Oh well. It had been fun. All adventures have to end at some point, right?

Apparently not.

"OH NO YOU DON'T!"

Captain Rick. Once my rival. Now my ally. The only man I knew who was crazy enough to leap off a wall to fight a dragon twenty times his size. He truly was nuts. Probably why I had so much respect for him.

He crashed into The Ender Dragon, his swords drawn. He slashed at its claws, causing it to lose its grip. Caught in the moment of his ridiculous heroics, it was only now I realized what was about to happen.

I prepared to jump myself, ready to grab him and pull him back from the portal, but The Commander wrapped an arm around my chest and refused to let go.

And incredibly, throughout everything, Captain Rick was smiling. The once evil Zombie Hunter turned hero. I can't believe I ever thought about scaring him.

"Let them all know the tale of Captain Rick, the greatest human who ever lived!" he yelled, laughing as he and The Ender Dragon collapsed into the portal, never to be seen again.

I'd be lying if I said I didn't cry a little.

Day 21

It has been a long time since the world has known peace.

There's always been something wrong with Minecraft. Whether it was simple things like humans building on a certain Zombie's property, or the most destructive creature ever born escaping its prison and wreaking havoc. There were always problems, popping up one after another.

Until now.

With the defeat of The Ender Dragon, the world has been saved. We now must walk the path of recovery. Overwatch is offering to help rebuild all the cities that were destroyed these past few days. And despite the loss of their Captain, the soldiers appear to be functioning well enough. The Commander has ordered them to help out with repairs for the time being.

I miss Rick. Despite our history, when we had the chance to work together, we became fast friends. And while I still have the scar he gave me, I don't hate him for it. Rather, I admire and respect him for his sacrifice. Still, knowing him he's probably fighting the Ender Dragon as we speak.

The Commander offered me a place here, and while the citizens may like me now, I can't stay. After all, there's a whole world out there to explore. And if I'm lucky, a cave with my name on it.

I'll come back one day. I've grown to love Overwatch after all. For now however, my destiny lies on the open road. Myself and Dave, if he wants to come along, still have plenty left to see and do.

I hope you've enjoyed my tale reader. However, this was only a single chapter in my life. Here's hoping you follow us until the very last page.

Signed,

Romero the Crafty Zombie

Book 4: Herobrine's Gauntlet

Prologue

Greetings mortals, and welcome to your demise!

Haha, just kidding. For now. Perhaps one day you'll be despawned at my hands, but for now I've got another story for you. You seem to have enjoyed the last few, so I might as well continue the trend. Anyways, welcome back dear reader. You've been missed.

So where does one go from here? I mean, we ended things last time with a Notch-like entity nearly destroying the planet. It really can't get more dangerous than that, right? Haha, oh man, you're going to be slapping yourself in a minute.

You see, Minecraft is home to some strange things. Good, bad and weird can be found all over this blocky planet. Today, we're going to be covering one of the bad things. Something that didn't just threaten one planet, but the entire universe itself.

Pretty serious, am I right? Bet I've got your attention now. Well, keep listening.

Tell me reader, you like stories. Ever hear the one about Herobrine's Gauntlet? I didn't think so. Well, you're about to find out.

And believe me when I say you'll wish you hadn't.

Day 1

Who dares to open my sacred diary?

Hehe, did I scare you? I always enjoy getting the drop on you blasted humans. Sure we might be good friends now, but old habits die hard. When I'm around, you'd best expect a jump scare or three. Anyways, if you've got your heart back in your chest, how's it going? Romero the Intelligent Zombie, at your service as always. And might I add it's great to be back.

Yes, we left things on a bit of a sour note, didn't we? Minecraft was nearly destroyed by Mr. Troll, a being known for his jokes gone too far. Sure we managed to beat him, but there was still the matter of fixing everything. Never before have I seen so many players working together to mine Cobblestone. Considering people normally have double chests for that stuff alone, the situation was pretty dire.

Anyways, skip ahead two years and things are looking up. The Enderman army used by that trollish dude is trapped in their dimension. Most of the damage has been repaired and we're looking at some cool new developments in the world. For example, top scientists have now discovered the method of holding two items… AT THE SAME TIME!

Yes, we'll finally be able to hold a sword in our left hand and a sword in our right hand. I can't believe it took them this long to figure it out (yes, there is a little bit of sarcasm in there BTW). Stupid science stuff aside, there's also been advancements in Redstone technology. We now have machines which can run without player input and can build entire structures. I'm pretty sure there's also been reports of giant robots fighting to the death. As cool as that would be, I'd rather not spend hours cleaning up the mess they leave

So yes, things are looking pretty great right now. And that's without mentioning the cool pyramids we've been discovering, but more on that later.

Minecraft has finally got the peace it deserves. No zombie hordes looking to destroy cities, no Ender Dragons swooping down from the sky and no pranksters who want to set the server on fire. For once, things are looking up.

At least, for now they are…

Day 2

Met with Commander Rick today.

Yes, that guy has just received a promotion. The old Commander has been through quite a bit these past few years, and decided to retire early. Of course, who better to give it to than good ol' Captain Rick? I mean, there was always me, but I think there's a rule about letting zombies run an army. Probably for the best, in hindsight.

We discussed future plans and such, trying to plot out our next move. Do we focus on rebuilding old cities or construct newer ones in their place? Do we send troops to clear out mob armies or keep them close to protect the citizens? Do we paint the walls green or pink? All difficult questions, each bringing their own consequences which could change the world as we know it.

We solved things as best we could, before retiring for the night. We weren't born to be leaders, but right now we're the best Minecraft has got. The men who were meant for this job are either fighting Ghasts in the Nether or don't care about what happens to the world. Sucks to be them, because we've got awesome jobs running the planet.

Oh whom am I kidding? It sucks. Just last week, we had to resolve an argument of 'who gets twelve cobblestone blocks found under a mountain'. A mountain made of cobblestone mind you.

You know, I can't say I miss having to save the world every five minutes, but I gotta say it was a lot more entertaining than this.

Day 3

Me and my big mouth.

So Rick and I had finally finished our work, and were deciding which restaurant to go to.

"Burger Bob's is pretty nice," Rick told me, "ate there with my girlfriend last week."

"I'm a vegetarian," I reminded him, "I quite fancy a nice salad."

"You're missing out on the best things in life Romero," Rick joked, but before I could shoot a retort back, we were interrupted by the arrival of a guard.

"Commander Rick, Councilor Romero, something terrible has happened!"

Yeah, they call me Councilor. Can't say I agree with it but oh well.

"What's wrong?" Rick had his hand on his sword in an instant.

"The explorers. Something's happened to them. They're not acting right…"

Exchanging a glance, my good human friend and I dashed outside, our weapons at the ready. The courtyard was full of soldiers, all gathered around three individuals dressed in leather gear. They wore patches of maps, signifying they were members of the Explorers Guild.

"HE'S COMING!" one of them screamed.

"THE EVIL ONE IS COMING!" cried another.

"HIDE YO KIDS, HIDE YO WIFE, 'CAUSE THE EVIL ONE IS COMING!"

They had truly gone insane.

We ended up dragging them inside and dousing water over their heads, which seemed to stop their rambling.

"Took long enough," Rick moaned, and I nodded. They'd been at it for twenty minutes.

"Apologies my lord," the head of the explorers spoke up. James, I believe his name was.

"What happened James?" I asked, kneeling down to examine him.

He didn't seem to like that, and he backed up immediately. I sighed. We zombies aren't known for having the nicest smelling breath.

"We… we discovered something in one of the temples you told us to investigate."

After Mr. Troll was found sleeping in a darned temple, Commander Rick decided to make sure that there weren't any more napping entities capable of ending life as we know it. A very decent move, if you ask me. Unfortunately, this also saw a rise in temple-related in injuries. Be it monsters or ancient artifacts, there have been a lot of respawning Explorers.

"What did you find?" I heard Rick whisper.

James glanced at his companions, pure fear in his eyes. At least, it looked like pure fear.

"Herobrine's Gauntlet."

Day 4

Gosh, as if things weren't ridiculous enough already.

I mean, we've already dealt with a rampaging Ender Dragon and a being that is the very definition of trolling. I like to think I'm pretty good at this whole 'saving the world thing now'. So when someone comes along and tells me they've discovered something that could be a bit of problem to the planet's health, I just put my boots on and order a takeaway when I'm done.

That's under normal circumstances of course. However, when someone comes up to me, claiming to possess an artifact of untold power, that's when I start to get a little bit worried. As is the case now.

Herobrine's Gauntlet. Described as the ultimate weapon. Rumor has it that Herobrine once arm-wrestled Notch while wearing it. The poor guy was in hospital for a week afterwards, on account of his hand looking like a cube.

Haha! Get it? Cuz our hands already look like cubes. Anyone? Anyone at all? Nope? Okay then.

The Explorers brought the glove back with them, which has since been stored in Overwatch's Vault. And before you complain, yes security has been beefed up. This won't end up like last time where world-ending artifacts get stolen.

Day 5

Someone tried stealing the world-ending artifact!

DON'T PANIC! I said tried. Keep it calm and keep it cool. Things are just fine. The guy who tried taking it is currently undergoing intense interrogation. By which I mean we're tickling him to find out what he knows. So far he's been fairly helpful.

His name is Chad and his favorite hobbies include reading, horseback riding and acquiring powerful weapons for people who are willing to pay lots of emeralds. His newest job was to break into The Vault and acquire Herobrine's Gauntlet. And while he may have made it past the laser defenses and the crocodiles, he was no match for the laser defense crocodile.

According to Chad, he was approached by a man in a cloak (why can't these people just dress normally?), who wanted him to steal Herobrine's Gauntlet. This raises many questions. Who is this mystery person? How did they find out about the Gauntlet? Why am I asking you when you know less than I do? All very important questions.

Once I have an answer, I'll get back to you. For now however, this looks like another detective mystery for Romero the Crafty Zombie to solve!

"And Commander Rick!"

Oh, sorry bud. This was kinda gonna be a solo mission. As in, something I solve all by myself.

"Please, you couldn't tell the difference between Dirt and Mycellium."

One's brown and the other's a purplish color?

"... Well played."

Anyway, I feel like you'll just slow me down Rick.

"I'll get you a bowl of your favorite mushroom soup."

Two bowls and a slice of carrot cake.

"Deal."

For now however, this looks like another detective mystery for Romero the Crafty Zombie and Rick the err... err... human?

"That's the best you could do?"

Silence sidekick!

Day 6

Romero and Rick are on the case.

We started things off by checking out the crime scene. The Vault. An old structure formed from finely cut Obsidian. The contents of this place include a sword which can turn people into sheep (very fun to use, I must say), a block of TNT that can't explode and a pork chop past its expiration date (which nearly poisoned a village to death).

The Gauntlet is protected by the finest defenses money can buy (including that awesome laser crocodile I mentioned), but Chad very nearly managed to steal it. If they send someone more competent, we might lose Herobrine's Gauntlet after all. And we're still not sure what it's capable of.

Sure, it made a bunch of the Explorers go a bit crazy, but other than that we're not sure what the true powers of this item are. I mean, if Herobrine himself made it then there has to be something other than turning people gaga.

Whatever it is, I intend to find out. Our search of

the vault didn't turn up much, but we're going to make sure that our enemies don't get another chance. We'll be taking the Gauntlet with us to assure its safety. So long as it doesn't try to possess us, I think we should be okay.

Hmm, we should probably find a way to stop that from happening.

Day 7

Rick has a plan.S

Today, we met up with Champion Steve. You guys remember him, right? Nice enough guy, protects the innocent, nearly helped Mr. Troll to win the final battle. He's a decent person, but sadly fell victim to a bit of possessive magic. Rick suggested we talk to him to see what the effects of being possessed are like.

"You don't realize you're being possessed," Steve explained, passing me a mug of water.

How very helpful.

"Technically, you can do whatever you please. The magic didn't stop me from acting normal and fighting to help free Minecraft. However, there were a few things to note. You guys noticed that I wrote my thoughts down in my diary. The ones that expressed my loyalty to Mr. Troll. Basically my body telling me what was actually going on."

"Anything else?" Rick inquired, even though he'd seen everything for himself.

"I thought you were the traitor, remember?" Steve reminded us, "I started suspecting those that I trusted of being the traitor. From my experience, the magic will probably try and find ways to impede you in anyway it can. If you wanted to destroy Herobrine's Gauntlet, it'd come up with all sorts of excuses. However, you're just looking for information. If I had to guess, it'll probably just want to get you on its side."

"So we're basically going to worship a glove?" I asked, sipping from my mug of water.

"Pretty much."

We said our goodbyes after that. Steve offered to do some research of his own, to which we happily agreed. He won't be joining us on our little adventure, but it's nice to know we've got someone back home who's going to help.

Right, the plan. I mentioned Rick had one, and he does. Basically a way of finding out just who we're dealing with.

"You want me to what?" Chad exclaimed.

After we'd finished questioning him, we allowed Chad to stay in a comfortable prison cell. He didn't have any more information to give us and we figured that he wouldn't try to escape, so there was no reason not to make things worse for him. Rick had also figured we might have need for him at some point. Of course he was right.

"You heard me," said the Commander, "I want you to lead us to the people who hired you."

"Out of the question," Chad shook his head, "you have no idea who you're messing with."

"Which is why we want to bring them down," I interrupted, "and we need your help for that."

"Forget it," Chad hissed, "you might as well imprison me again, because there is no way in the Nether that I'm leading you to these people."

"I'll give you a stack of diamond blocks."

"What time do we leave?'" asked Chad.

Day 8

Operation Anti-Herobrine Squad has begun!

Man, I just love coming up with operation names. After all, who is better suited to the task than Romero the Crafty Zombie? Crafter of cool items and even cooler names.

"Romero, will you keep it down back there?" Rick demanded, "I am trying to drive this darned Minecart."

Jeez, that man can be grouchy when he hasn't had his morning coffee. Eh, whatever. We're currently en route to Megablockz, the city where (according to Chad), he was hired to steal Herobrine's Gauntlet.

"These guys came to my hideout," he explained, "normally if someone wants something stolen, they have to find another way to contact me. You don't just find out where I live. I'm a very careful individual."

"Somehow I doubt that," Rick sighed, swerving to avoid crashing into another Minecart.

So they managed to find Chad's house. Hardly the

most dangerous of enemies if they're able to follow someone back home. Still, we'll have to keep his warnings in mind about these people being incredibly dangerous. Who knows what they've got up their sleeve?

Actually, do they even have sleeves? We don't know a single thing about them. Not even a name. Chad groaned when I asked him about this.

"I don't know the names of their members, but I do know the name of the group," he explained, "they're known as the Cult of Herobrine."

Really? Surely not? I never would have expected the Cult of Herobrine to be after an item by the name of 'Herobrine's Gauntlet'. There's no way they'd ever be interested in something like that.

"Alright, I get the sarcasm," Chad hissed, "but it's true."

"Hate to burst your bubble kid," Rick spoke up, "but the Cult of Herobrine is no more. They've been destroyed."

"And how to do you know that?" I questioned.

"Because I was the one who brought them down."

Now that was interesting. Still, I was kind of annoyed that Rick had accomplished another amazing feat. I mean jeez, this guy was turning out to be a bigger hero than I was. Saved Overwatch from the Ender Dragon, fought said Ender Dragon for weeks on end and surviving to tell the tale, and now I hear he took out some evil cult.

FYI, the Cult of Herobrine is really bad news. Without going into too much detail, they're known to possess destructive magical powers that really mess with people. One example would be overcooking their food. Another might be to put a dent in someone's Minecart. Truly despicable and evil acts.

"So let's pretend they're still around for a second," I said, ignoring the glare Rick was giving me, "why do they want Herobrine's Gauntlet?"

"Isn't it obvious?" Chad asked us both, to which we shook our heads.

"They want to bring him back."

Day 9

Bring back Herobrine?

Impossible. There was no way they were going to resurrect one of the Creators in Minecraft. Maybe Chad was trying to trick us or maybe the Cult of Herobrine had tricked him. At any rate, there wasn't a chance in the Nether they'd be bringing him back.

The Creators are long gone. Notch and Herobrine both passed away a very long time ago, and Mr. Troll just got his rear end handed to him. The only reason he showed up was because he'd been sealed away, rather than destroyed.

Anyways, enough of my boring explanations. We've arrived in Megablockz and have checked into a hotel. Nothing too fancy, considering we want to save our money.

"Here you are gentlemen," the manager led us into the penthouse, "the five-star penthouse suite with the finest room service money can buy. That will be a heck of a lot of emeralds."

IT EVEN HAS A HOT TUB!

"I've got this," Chad whispered, handing the man a sack filled with the rare resource, "keep the change."

"Thank you sir," the manager beamed, walking out of the room.

I was utterly speechless, even more so when the thief revealed what he was holding in his hand. A bag twice the size of the one he'd given the manager.

"How did you…"

"I'm a thief, remember?" Chad winked, "Now let's get down to business. Only reason I'm helping you guys is so I can get these cult guys off my back. Still, there's no reason we can't enjoy ourselves while we're doing it."

He had a point. What better way to hunt down our foes than in style? We'd go explore the city, kick bad guy butt and proceed to chill here for the rest of the evening. Talk about living the easy life.

Day 10

This may be slightly more difficult than I realized.

Chad left earlier today to meet with one of the members of the Cult of Herobrine. Rick tailed him to make sure he didn't sell us out to these whack jobs, while I stayed here and made sure the apartment was 'safe'.

I ordered room service three times, bounced on the beds and even had a pillow fight with the Skeletons in the opposite room. The hours ticked by slowly, and I soon found myself without anything to do. Just what was taking Chad and Rick so long?

I got my answer a few minutes later, with the Commander bursting through the door. He was clutching his shoulder.

"What happened?" I asked him, glancing over his injuries.

"They ambushed us," Rick moaned, reaching for a health potion in one of the cabinets, "There must have been two dozen of them, all wielding swords, bows and even magic."

So these guys did have magical powers, and appeared to be fairly dangerous. Guess Chad had been telling the truth. Speaking of which…

"Where is Chad?"

Rick shook his head, "We got separated and I heard screaming. I think they got him. Doesn't matter. We have to get out of here. We really are dealing with some nasty players here."

And that's when the penthouse exploded.

Day 11

Don't worry, we're alive!

Haha, bet you were scared for a second. The great Romero and the slightly-less great Rick, defeated by an exploding hotel. Don't be ridiculous. It will take a lot more than that to drop our hearts to zero.

Nope, we're perfectly fine. Great even. Sure we've had to flee the city while being pursued by some of the most powerful and destructive people we've ever encountered, but we're doing great. Amazingly even. I must say I've never felt this –

Ah, whom am I kidding? We're sleeping under a bunch of trees, taking turns to keep watch. Most of our supplies were vaporized in the explosion and to top it all off, my wig was half burnt off.

Yes, I wear a wig. Most people aren't used to a talking, intelligent zombie, so I often have to pass myself off as a human. Doesn't take too much work, just a fake hairpiece and some makeup. In fact, I've never looked better.

More on my fashion tips later, but right now we've got bigger problems. We've indeed confirmed that the Cult of Herobrine is still around and are actively hunting us down. Most likely for Herobrine's Gauntlet, which is completely and utterly useless.

Yes, we tried using it against the Cult of Herobrine. Probably a stupid move, but whatever. We were expecting it to shoot lasers or call down a meteor from the sky to crush our foes, yet it did absolutely nothing. We ended up throwing Cobblestone at them instead. Much more effective.

So now we're without help, trying to evade capture from deadly sorcerers and are running low on supplies. Why does this stuff always happen to the good guys?

Day 12

Good news at long last!

We've received a message from Steve. We actually woke up this morning to a bird attacking our faces. I briefly considered turning it into our lunch, when two things happened.

1.   I remembered I was a vegetarian.

2.   I noticed it was carrying a letter.

After restraining Commander Rick so he didn't eat the bird, I removed the letter from its leg and allowed it to leave.

"COME BACK HERE YOU DELICIOUS BEAST!" Rick chased after it, as I began reading.

Dear Romero and Rick,

I hope you are both faring well on your quest. Knowing you guys, you've probably already defeated the bad guys (who I assume you've figured out are the Cult of Herobrine). On the off chance you haven't however, and had your rear ends handed to you, I have some information that may be of use.

As Rick has probably mentioned, Romero, he was sent on a mission a while back to destroy the Cult of Herobrine. Although he succeeded, it appears enough members escaped to reform the group. We're not sure how, but they also appear to have gained new powers, making them much more deadly than last time.

The Cult of Herobrine is after Herobrine's Gauntlet. In the past, this object was used by Herobrine himself to resurrect fallen Minecraft players. All the Zombies and Skeletons that exist today were actually created by this item. Another look through 'Important Story Information' tells me that Herobrine's Gauntlet is rumored to contain a piece of his soul.

Rick and Romero, it is vital you do not allow the Cult to obtain Herobrine's Gauntlet. If they do, they may have the ability to resurrect him. And the last thing we need is that guy hanging around. Mr. Troll was bad enough.

If you're stuck for clues and want to find out more about the Gauntlet, I think I know where you can start looking. A few thousand blocks North-East of Megablockz, you'll find another long lost temple. This one was next on the Explorer's Guild's list, but they're still unfit for travel. I suggest you get over there before someone else does.

Finally, there's something you should know. Strange things have been happening at Overwatch. People are going missing and there are odd noises at night. The *other champions and I have gone to look for them, but so far our search has turned up nothing. If the Cult is behind this, rest assured they will be brought to justice.*

Take care of yourselves guys. I feel this is just the beginning of something much greater.

Champion Steve

"It got away," Rick eventually returned, a sad look on his face. I passed him the letter without another word. He read it in silence, his eyebrows going up and down in shock.

"Herobrine's soul? Another long lost temple? Champion Steve?"

"It's all very shocking," I agreed, nodding, "but we have to get moving. The Cult is still after us, and we can't let them beat us there."

"Agreed," Rick nodded, "we'll saddle up the horses and ride immediately."

"We don't have any horses," I reminded him, to which he grinned.

"But we will."

Oh dear. I know that grin all too well.

Day 13

You will not believe the day I just had.

Did you know that Commander Rick keeps a pair of 'emergency saddles' in his back pocket, in case a situation ever arose where he needed two horses and didn't have his Minecart. Apparently, the same thing has happened once before and since then, he's decided to prepare himself for any and all future events. He also carries an 'emergency fire-making kit', an 'emergency arrow' and of course, an 'emergency sandwich'.

Which I ate last night, but don't tell him that.

Anyways, Rick 'conveniently' came down with a cold and a case of 'bad leg', so he asked me to capture the horses for him. I disagreed, and thus followed

"COUGH, COUGH, COUGH, COUGH!" He spluttered and wheezed and sneezed.

"OW, OW, OW!" He moaned and groaned and clutched his limb.

Honestly, I think I went to find the horses because

Rick was annoying me so much. What followed was a hunt that took at least fifteen minutes of my precious time, before I finally stumbled upon a clearing with two beautiful looking horses.

"Alright, let's get this over with," I mumbled to myself.

Now normally with humans, they have to ~~right click~~ climb on the horse numerous times before the animal likes it enough. A strange technique, I know. Fortunately, I have a much better solution.

"YAAAAAAH!" I screamed, leaping onto the back of one of the mounts.

In hindsight, it was a terrible idea.

I was immediately thrown backwards into a tree, whereupon I lay for several minutes while my battered body recovered. Translation: it hurt a heck of a lot. I quickly tried again however. And again. And again. And again. After a few minutes, it soon became apparent that my idea just wasn't working out.

I'm ashamed to admit I ended up using the human technique in the end. Climbing on the horse, getting knocked off and then climbing on it again. It took a while, but eventually I'd managed to tame one of them and fit a saddle on him.

I was dreading the taming of the other one, when Commander Rick limped over to me.

"What's the problem?" he asked, "You seem to be taking your time."

"You try getting these things to like you," I hissed.

He raised an eyebrow, before pulling out an 'emergency apple' and feeding it to the second horse. He saddled it immediately afterwards.

I was in absolute shock. My jaw had hit the floor. Rick just gave me a smug grin and started riding off.

Oh one of these days, I'll get him back.

Day 14

We arrived at the temple.

An old structure made of stone and consumed by vines. The entire place was infested with all sorts of nasty creatures, ranging from Cave Spiders to Wither Skeletons. Mobs you don't tend to see on the surface.

"This place is definitely strange," said Rick, as a pair of monsters he cut down disappeared in a cloud of smoke.

I agreed, quickly convincing an ugly looking zombie that we weren't walking happy meals. Sure does help to speak their languages. After making our way through a few more opponents, we managed to reach the temple entrance.

"Keep your guard up," Rick cautioned, removing a torch from his backpack and lighting it. Our last.

And so began our descent into the depths of Minecraftia. There wasn't much to say about the temple. It might once have been a place to worship Herobrine, but right now it was little more than a crumbling structure with little to nothing inside. Cobwebs stained the walls and the whole place looked it could collapse at any second.

Rick seemed to read my mind, "Herobrine's temple? This place looks like it's been abandoned for centuries. I'm guessing the cult didn't know about it. They probably wouldn't be too happy to know their Creator's building is in such disrepair."

The journey continued. We reached a massive staircase, taking us into the heart of the temple. There were no monsters to be found here, and the area actually looked… clean? Like someone had taken the time to make sure it looked nice.

"I don't like this," I whispered to Rick, "what if someone HAS been here?"

"Looks like we're about to find out…"

We finally reached the end of the staircase, leading to a small room lit by torches. Someone had obviously been here. At the center of this small tomb was an old stone table and a small chest.

"This looks eerily similar to what Steve described to us," Rick recalled, "be very careful…"

I nodded, approaching the chest on the tablet. Taking a deep breath to steady myself, I opened it with a shaking hand. Thankfully, there wasn't any evil spirit inside. Just a red crystal.

"LOOT!" I yelled, removing it from the chest and examining it. It was small, but looked to be worth a pretty penny at a marketplace.

And that's when I noticed the strange indents on Herobrine's Gauntlet. Little markings, like they would house an object of some kind.

"Rick, come look at this," I motioned him over, indicating the gauntlet and the stone.

"Don't tell me you're thinking of doing that..."

"But what if it helps us?" I questioned, "what if this is what we've been searching for? Answers that could help us in our fight. Imagine using the cult's own weapon against them!"

Rick stroked his imaginary beard for a minute, locked in his thoughts as decisions weighed themselves in his mind.

"Alright," he nodded, "but be careful."

"I will, I promise."

And with that, I inserted the stone into the gauntlet. A bright flash of light followed soon afterwards, followed by the smell of burnt chicken.

"Gah, what in the blazes was that?"

That voice... it didn't belong to Rick or I. And I'm fairly certain we didn't bring any guests with us.

The light faded and the smell soon faded. Once my sight had returned, I began scanning the room for the disturbance. I soon located it. Rick was lying on his back, clutching his side with a pained expression on his face. And standing above him was…

"BOW BEFORE YOUR MASTER, MORTALS!" Herobrine roared, his white eyes glowing, "FOR HEROBRINE LIVES ONCE MORE!"

Book 5: The Cult of Herobrine

Prologue

Well hello there, and welcome back to my little adventure.

Yes, you are once again reading the epic and mind-boggling tales, straight from the mind of Romero. Crafty Zombie and Minecraft Veteran. I've saved the world more times than I can count, I've invented a hundred and twenty-seven ways to butter toast and I've even played a card game with a penguin. And what have you been doing with your summer holiday?

Ah whatever, they'll be time to discuss boring things later. For now, let's talk about something much more exciting. Something like, I don't know, me. Yeah, that's an interesting topic. I quite like that. Let's talk some more about Romero.

COUGH! COUGH!

Fine, and my sidekick Commander Rick.

"Sidekick? We've been over this. I'm your partner. We're equals!"

Pretty sure I've saved the world more times than you have.

"So?"

Pretty sure I've also got more brain cells too.

"Why you little…"

Right, back to the matter at hand. When we last left, we'd successfully summoned Herobrine back to the world of the living. Spoiler alert if you haven't read the previous book.

"What's the point in putting a spoiler alert AFTER the spoiler?"

Don't question it! At any rate, my 'partner' and I were face to face with the most demonic entity known to man…

"A Spider Jockey?"

Zip it.

"Oh, have we reached the part where you and I were suspended-"

SPOILERS! Jeez, and apparently I'm the bad one. Still, welcome back reader, to what could very well be our final adventure. And I really mean it this time. I know we often get into lots of danger, only to escape at the very last minute, but let me assure you that this is the most dangerous undertaking in the history of Minecraft. I don't know about you, but I'd say that's pretty unsafe for my health.

"Unsafe for you maybe, but not the great and mighty Commander Rick!"

Right, that's it.

"What are you... no, not the duct tape. MERCY!"

Day 1

Do you guys have a bucket list?

I know I have one. There's nothing I enjoy more than completing things on this particular list. Gives me a sense of accomplishment. Makes me feel awesome! I've done many things to fulfil it, from riding off a mountain on a pig to saving the world eighty two and a half times. Granted, I've probably saved it a BIT more than that at this point.

One thing that is noticeably absent on my bucket list however is summoning the ancient spirit of the most evil entity in Minecraft's history. I did consider putting it on there at one point, but decided against it. Too much clean up if it decides to destroy the world.

At any rate, I seem to have done just that…

"BORN AGAIN TO WREAK TERROR UPON THE EARTH!" Herobrine cried, his form manifesting within the tomb, "KNEEL MORTALS, AND PERHAPS I SHALL SPARE YOU LONG ENOUGH TO WATCH YOUR WORLD BURN!"

"We'll see about that," Commander Rick threatened, lunging forward and swinging his sword, aiming to bring an end to Herobrine in one, swift blow...

The blade never connected, instead passing right through him.

"Huh?" I scratched my head, confused for the first time in my life. Rick also scratched his, but I'm guessing he's been confused a lot more times.

"WHAT IS THE MEANING OF THIS!?" Herobrine demanded, "WHY IS MY PHYSICAL FORM REFUSING TO MANIFEST?"

As he bellowed and yelled, attempting to smash up the chamber in the process (his fists passing through everything), Rick and I marched up to the chest. We noticed something we'd missed before: a small scrap of paper. Exchanging a glance, we picked it up and began reading.

THANK YOU FOR YOUR PURCHASE OF ONE RED POWER CRYSTAL, DESIGNED TO RESURRECT THE SPIRIT OF HEROBRINE. TO USE, PLEASE INSERT RED POWER CRYSTAL INTO HEROBRINE'S GAUNTLET. BATTERY LIFE: TEN THOUSAND YEARS. FOR RECHARGING, YOU MUST ALSO PURCHASE ONE BLUE AND ONE GREEN POWER CRYSTAL. CHARGING STATIONS CAN BE FOUND AT YOUR LOCAL HEROBRINE TEMPLE. THANK YOU FOR SHOPPING AT HEROBRINE'S STORE!

Talk about bad luck... for Herobrine, that is.

We decided to get the heck out of there while the ghost was busy moaning and groaning. After all, if he's stuck in that form, he's no trouble to us. It was the perfect opportunity to return home for some delicious mushroom soup.

Unfortunately, we weren't expecting to run into the Cult of Herobrine.

Day 2

Out of the fire, and into the frying pan.

Yes, we've been nabbed by those darned cultists. Two-dozen of them had been waiting outside the temple. Apparently they aren't allowed to step into the 'sacred grounds of Herobrine', lest they get dirt on his 'fantastic floor'. They really are insane.

Dressed in purple robes and hiding behind hoods, they dragged us for a good few hundred blocks before we got to our destination. A wooden fortress of some kind, hidden deep within the forest. The perfect place to brew up some evil scheme if you didn't want to get caught.

Bad news is they threw us in a cell and stole most of our gear, including Herobrine's Gauntlet. Speaking of that evil creep…

"HOW DARE YOU CALL ME SUCH A NAME!"

Yeah, he's still around. I'm not sure how it works exactly, but he's 'bound to my soul'?

"You should be honored to be in such a position.

For me, it is utterly humiliating…"

Poor baby. Yes, I'm being haunted by Herobrine. Rick finds the whole thing really amusing, though I'm personally annoyed of his whining and somewhat confused. The cultists have the gauntlet, so why isn't Herobrine hanging out with them?

"Get us out of here and I might tell you," he shrugged, "either way, these guys are a little too creepy for my liking."

Too creepy for Herobrine? What have we gotten ourselves into?

We need a plan to escape. Fortunately, being the genius that I am, I've already come up with four.

"Herobrine, I need you to go deliver a message to a friend," I told the spirit.

"HAH!" he laughed, "You have friends? Sorry not sorry. But do carry on."

"Can you visit Steve in Overwatch? He's the leader of the Minecraft Champions. Get him to come and rescue us."

"I… can't…" Herobrine muttered.

"And why not?" I inquired.

"I'm bound to you. Technically I'm not allowed to stray fifty blocks away without your permission."

Sigh.

"Fine, I give you my permission to leave to deliver this message to Steve."

"Alright!"

"And once you're done, you have to come back here."

"Gosh dang it."

Hehe. There's something fun about being able to control the most demonic creation in Minecraft's history. Still, had to make sure he'd show up afterwards and not wander around. Even if he is a spirit, I can still see him stirring up trouble.

For now, the only thing Rick and I can do is wait. Either for Steve and the others to rescue us, or for an opportunity to escape ourselves...

Day 3

We had a visitor to the cells today!

I hate visitors.

It was none other than the cultist leader. I figured this because his robes were a different color to the rest of his followers. Pro-tip bro: red robes haven't been in fashion for at least three updates.

"Do you know who I am?" he asked us, two of his pals standing at his left and right.

"By any chance are you our rescuers?" Rick inquired, a grin on his face.

"Your funny friend will be Herobrine's first meal, if he keeps up that attitude," the cultist threatened, "now answer my question."

"Buddy," I raised my hand, "I don't know if you're aware of how things work around here, so I'll explain it to you in a nice, simple manner. I'm the funny guy. He's the sidekick. Understand?"

Red Robes glared at me, a red fire burning in his red eyes.

"So you are the one who dares to force Herobrine to submit to his will…"

"Doesn't that mean you guys should worship me?" I questioned, "I mean, Herobrine does do what I want now. Pretty sure he's currently rummaging through all your closets and messing up your clothes."

"You dare to mock the great and mighty Herobrine?" Red Robes hissed, "You are fortunate I don't strike you down where you sit. Most fortunate indeed."

"If it gets me out of listening to you, then please do strike me down."

"RARGH!"

Red Robes stormed out of the tent, his lackeys following him. Before he left however, he gave us one final warning.

"Herobrine will not be controlled by you forever, mortal. When he breaks free, he shall spare only those he deems worthy. Making him play pranks won't make you any friends."

And with that, he left, leaving me with a growing sense of worry. Herobrine breaking free? Alright, I suppose it's possible, but what's he going to do afterwards? Haunt me for the rest of his life? Haha, hilarious.

So long as he doesn't have a body, we'll be just fine.

Day 4

Oh sweet mother of biscuits, anything but that!

So remember when I said Herobrine doesn't have a body and as long as he doesn't get his hands on one, we'll have no problems whatsoever?

It turns out the Cult of Herobrine specializes in putting spirits in physical forms. Who would have guessed that a group dedicated to bringing Herobrine back to life actually has a way of bringing him back to life?

Sarcasm aside, we need to get out of here. Only reason we know this is because Ol' Red Robes came in and specifically told Commander Rick he'd be the lucky victim.

"But why not Romero? He's much younger AND he's the funny one!" he protested.

"Leave me out of this!" I hissed.

"We'd rather not drop our master into a zombie body. We have a feeling he wouldn't be too happy with that."

Well, that's nice. Herobrine should be honored to have a body such as mine.

"As soon as Herobrine returns from whatever stupid errand the undead sent him on, we shall begin the ritual. Enjoy your body while you still control it, Commander."

Red Robes marched off out of the cells, leaving poor Rick to sob in the corner and mutter to himself. Something along the lines of: "Not me. Anyone but me. Why not Romero? The world could live without his jokes."

Nice to know who your true friends are. Well, seeing as Rick isn't up to the task, it's up to me to find a way out of here!

Day 5

So here's how the escape plan was going to work.

I was hidden in the darkened corner of the cell, waiting for the jailor to collect our dirty plates. Soggy black bread for dinner by the way. Not the tastiest meal I've ever had. Anyways, the plan was to knock the jailor out, steal his uniform and hightail it out of there.

A sound plan of course, especially since I came up with it. So I waited by the door, a block of dirt in hand, planning to hit the jailor over the head as soon as he entered the room.

And he did. The door swung open and the armored man marched in, carrying a tray and a bowl of Mushroom Soup.

"YARGH!" I cried, striking him and knocking him to the floor.

"OW, MY SPLEEN!" the guard cried, in a surprisingly familiar tone.

Before I could act on it however, Rick sprang from

his own corner and began hitting the poor guy with my diary. If this page looks a little torn, you now know why.

"WHAT ARE YOU DOING?" I bellowed, removing the object from his hand.

"Was I too rough?" Rick asked.

"No you idiot," I hissed, shaking my head, "you could wreck the diary. I spent weeks making this thing."

"You got it at the General Store," Rick reminded me.

"Oh yeah."

"Are you idiots done arguing!?"

Oh dear. That tone. That voice. That could only belong to one person. With a shaking hand, I removed the helmet of the 'guard'.

"By Notch's beard, what did you do that for?" Champion Viktor demanded.

Viktor. The Champion of Lightning and Wielder of the Storm Hammer. Tended to get very angry if you tried knocking him out.

"What are you doing here?" Rick asked, helping Viktor to his feet.

"Isn't it obvious idiot? I'm here to rescue you. The other Champions have the guards distracted, but we have to get moving before-"

"STOP RIGHT THERE!"

At the end of the hall stood two of Herobrine's servants, fireballs floating around their heads. Viktor wasted no time in emerging from the cell and smacking his hammer into the ground.

"LIGHTNING HAMMER!"

His technique had certainly improved since I last saw him use that move. The hallway practically crumbled as the electrical attack sped forward, tearing up the floor and collapsing the walls. It dashed the two cultists into the opposite end of the room, leaving them unconscious.

"Let's go," Viktor led us out of the cells and back to the surface up a wooden staircase. Amy, Champion of Archery and Wielder of Dinnerbone's Crossbow, stood waiting for us, firing the occasional arrow at our foes. When she spotted us, she shot us a grin and threw us some familiar looking objects. My Blade of End and Rick's double swords.

"Nice to see you guys are in one piece," she winked, blasting a few more projectiles at the cultists. A short distance away, I spotted Champions Steve and Winston fighting side by side, taking on Red Robes. I was wondering why none of his subjects were trying to help, before I spotted Champion Boris chasing them down with his giant stick.

"Looks like you guys made mincemeat of them," Rick chuckled, joining in the fight. In a few short seconds, he'd knocked down two of the Cult of Herobrine and engaged a third in a sword battle.

"What took you guys so long?" I asked Amy, "Do you have any idea what they've been feeding us?"

"Surprisingly, we were a little reluctant to follow Herobrine," the female Champion retorted, "He's not known to be the most trustworthy type."

"Point taken."

"ENOUGH OF THIS!"

A wave of magic propelled Steve and Winston into a conveniently placed haystack. Red Robes was marching towards us, his arms glowing with some sort of purple energy.

"You will not stop the return of Herobrine. I shall dispose of the lot of you, and bring my master back to the physical plane of existence. Your time here is done!"

"Not if I have anything to stay about it!"

Rick joined the fray, twirling his twin swords and aiming for his target's head. Red Robes ducked, thrusting his palm forward and knocking Rick to his rear end. The cultist followed up with some form of fire spell, but the Commander cut it in half with one sword and fired his own spell with his second sword.

"Ancient Seals!"

Several strands of rope shot from the blade, twirling around Red Robes. He struggled and fought against them, attempting to wiggle himself free. Rick just grinned, before echoing his next attack.

"JUDGEMENT STRIKE!"

His blades glowing a blinding white, he brought them down in an X-formation, leaving burning streaks across Red Robes' body. He then turned, spinning his swords and throwing his opponent through one of the buildings with the flat end of the blades. The wooden wall immediately shattered upon impact.

"NICE ONE!" we all cheered for our ally, who could only bow in response. Maybe he was worth partner material after all.

"You dare…"

Or maybe not.

Red Robes emerged from the building, his clothing torn from where Rick had slashed him. His fists were clenched and there was true, burning anger in his eyes.

"We'll all attack him at once," I told the other Champions, "there's no way he'll escape a combined strike."

"Fools, you cannot destroy me," Red Robes taunted, "I am beyond your power. I am the very embodiment of Herobrine himself."

"That's kind of offensive."

Herobrine himself had at last decided to appear,

leaning casually against a building, before comically falling through it. Guess he was still getting used to being a spirit.

"My apologies my master," Red Robes knelt down, "I meant no offense. However, I must inform your… companions that if they do decide to attack me, they lose any chance of stopping your return."

Wait, what?

"What do you mean?" I asked, pointing the Blade of Ender at my foe. One blast and I could have him transported to that terrible dimension.

"What I mean is that I'd planned for this. Did you really think I believed you sent my master off to prank us? I knew he had to be fetching help for you, so I decided to accelerate my plans. Tell me undead, do you think you've taken down the entire cult?"

I glanced over the collection of unconscious and injured bodies. They would really be feeling ill in the morning. A quick headcount confirmed my fears. Twenty-three. Aside from Red Robes, there had been two-dozen loyal servants to Herobrine's cause.

"My second-in-command is already making his way to the second gem. He has Herobrine's Gauntlet and the red gem with him. Once he had his hands on the blue power crystal, Herobrine will be one step closer to returning."

"TAKE HIM DOWN!" Herobrine ordered, "And not just because we won't be able to stop his friend. I, err, don't like his beard."

"Then I shall shave it my master," Red Robes declared, removing a knife and slashing the beard off in one cut.

"Tell us where your second-in-command is," Rick demanded.

"On one condition. I walk away."

I glanced at the other Champions. Each of them looked uncomfortable (especially Winston and Steve, considering the wall they'd just 'hugged), but refused to speak. Rick was the Commander, and it was his decision to make.

"...Fine," Rick muttered, "Now tell us where he is."

Red Robes grinned, clicking his fingers. A tear in the fabric of reality (also known as a portal) appeared by his side, to which he stepped into.

"The Museum of the Fallen, Commander," Red Robes spoke, "my second-in-command will be stealing the power crystal shortly. I suggest you hurry, if you plan on stopping him."

And before another word could be spoken, he'd vanished, along with his gateway.

"Museum of the Fallen?" Steve asked, to which most of the others shrugged. Rick however, looked off into the distance.

"We're heading to Oldtown."

Day 6

If there's one thing I don't know about Rick, it's his past.

He doesn't talk about it much. Yeah, I know he was once a bounty hunter. He used to go after all sorts of dangerous targets, including some of the nastiest zombies around. Over the past two years, I've gotten to know plenty of his exploits over bowls of Mushroom Soup. A great way to keep us entertained when we were bored as heck.

However, there was one story he didn't talk much about. Scratch that, one he never talked about. His mission to Oldtown. All I knew were the rumors you sometimes heard in the barracks. That Commander Rick (at the time, Hunter) had headed to Oldtown with a partner of some kind. He'd returned to Overwatch a few days later to collect his payment. Alone.

I'd never asked him about it, out of respect. But looking at him now, I can see something is bothering him. A troubling thought that's distracting him, and could get him injured if things stay like this. I'll have to keep an eye on him, just to make sure nothing happens.

Last thing I want is to return to Overwatch without my Commander.

Anyways, we've made our way out of that wooden fort (which we of course burnt to the ground) and had some of the Overwatch soldiers arrest the cultists and lock them up. They won't be troubling us anymore, but we still have two members unaccounted for.

Steve reckons if we capture this 'second-in-command', then he'll lead us to Red Robes. With the two of them dealt with, we can put an end to this Cult of Herobrine once and for all.

"Do I even have a say in this?" Herobrine moaned.

Nope.

The soldiers have supplied us with horses. Oldtown is only a day's ride away. I just hope we can make it in time.

Day 7

Oldtown.

A bastion of knowledge and wisdom. If Overwatch is the strongest city, then Oldtown is the smartest. Not sure how a city can be smart, but eh. People from all over Minecraft come to study here and learn all sorts of skills and techniques. From crafting to smithing and even learning the language of Zombish. If you want to learn something, Oldtown is the place to go.

"Keep your hood up," Rick cautioned, "Overwatch is used to you Romero, but I don't see these students reacting all that well."

I agreed, throwing on my hood and gloves and keeping my head down. The four champions had me concealed in a circle-like formation, waving anyone on who tried to take a closer look.

"So what is the Museum of the Fallen?" Amy asked.

"A museum for people who fall over," Viktor

chuckled.

"Moron," Winston sighed, "it's a museum dedicated to the Pre-Alpha age. It has relics of all the fallen Heroes and Champions who sought to protect the planet from the darkest of evils."

"Correct," Rick nodded, "Back then, Herobrine used to be on the side of good."

"Don't remind me," I'd ordered Herobrine to render himself invisible, but I could imagine he had his arms crossed right now, "it was a terrible mistake on my part."

"Don't suppose you'd be willing to share any information?" Steve asked.

"About the Pre-Alpha age?" Herobrine asked, "Let's just say that Red Robes was little more than a grain of sand, compared to what we had to fight."

He didn't look it right now, but the stories stated that Herobrine had been the second greatest warrior the world had ever seen, only bested by Notch himself. I wonder what made him decide to turn coat and join the forces of evil.

I didn't have time to daydream any longer, as we were coming up on the museum. A grand and mighty structure, with beautiful windows and stern-looking guards.

"Welcome to the museum," one of the staff members emerged from the structure, accompanied by the heavily armored defenders, "we welcome all visitors, though we must ask that you leave your weapons with our security personnel."

"Are you the curator?" I asked. The man nodded.

"Yes. Can I help you gentlemen with something?"

"I'm Romero, Leader of Overwatch, we have reason to believe that a break-in will take place in the museum very shortly, and we must insist that we set a trap for the criminal."

"And why on earth should I believe that?"

I glanced at Rick, who nodded. I clicked my fingers and removed my hood.

I don't know what shocked the curator more. The talking zombie or the spirit of Herobrine. Whatever it was, it caused him to pass out.

"Well we're off to a fine start," Steve chuckled.

Indeed we were.

Day 8

Okay, it took some explaining but I'm pretty sure we've got everything all figured out.

The Curator was a little weary at first, and seemed to have a hard time to take everything in. Probably because he knocked his noggin when he collapsed. But with an icepack in hand and a good few hours listening to us, we're fairly certain he understood what was going on.

"So an evil being that nearly destroyed the world thousands of years ago has been brought back as a spirit, but is now under your control. Meanwhile, a cult dedicated to said spirit is determined to revive him, but the only way they can do that is by stealing the power crystal we have stored at the museum. Therefore, in order to stop him, you need to have total control of the museum to set a trap for this thief?"

A pause for a second. Two. Then…

"Pretty much," Viktor gave The Curator a thumbs up, who sighed in response.

"Oh very well," he muttered, "Sorry, Commander Rick, I did not notice before that you were with Romero. I know your valor. You've protected this planet numerous times, and as long as you promise no harm will come to the exhibits, I give you my permission to do as you please."

"Many thanks Curator," Rick shook the man's hand, as did I, though he immediately washed his hands after I touched them.

"I'll close the museum for the next few days," the Curator continued, "that should attract the thief. I also offer you use of the apartment on the top floor until this business is dealt with."

Excellent. That left us with enough time to get set-up AND a place to chill. A nice change to the 'uncomfortable living conditions' we'd experienced the past few days.

"Oh, and Rick?"

As we were leaving, the Curator called out once more.

"I trust things will go better than last time."

Last time?

Rick only slammed the door in response, before marching off to his room.

Day 9

Last time?

We'd spent the day preparing for the visitor. To start things off, we investigated the museum. A really nice looking place, complete with all sorts of cool exhibits. Skeletons of creatures who'd perished long ago. Strange looking weapons and armor, formed out of some material called 'steel'. Even sponge blocks! Truly an amazing sight.

The blue power crystal was located in one of the furthest rooms, adorned on some pedestal. A couple of guards stood by it, but they waved us by once they saw us.

We replaced the crystal with a fake. In case we did fail, the thief wouldn't get their hands on anything. Of course, we weren't here for failure. So we also set up a bunch of laser activated lava-traps, motion-sensing dispensers which shot arrows and of course, a giant axe. Because what trap is complete without a giant axe?

With that done, the Champions began patrolling the museum. When I offered to accompany them, Steve shook his head.

"Go see Rick," he told me, "something's bothering the guy."

So I wasn't the only one who'd noticed. And of course, there was what The Curator had said that had really agitated Rick. I told Herobrine to stick with the Champions, before I went looking for the Commander.

I found him looking over the balcony in our room. He was staring at the streets below, watching the people go about their daily lives, unaware of the threat that loomed over their very heads.

"This isn't the first time I've been here," Rick told me as I stepped beside him, staring at the city below.

"I heard," I nodded, "lots of stories that go around the barracks."

Rick grunted, "Figures. Soldiers don't know when to keep their mouths shut."

"They don't know the whole thing," I pointed out, "just bits and pieces."

"Fair enough, I never did tell anyone the whole story."

We stood in silence for a few minutes. I was curious, but wasn't going to push him to tell me.

"Myself and a good friend of mine, Leon… we were sent to Oldtown on a bounty hunting mission. Nothing too serious, we just had to apprehend a sorcerer who was causing mischief. We arrived here, started asking around for information, before The Curator told us that he'd seen the sorcerer in the Library of Ancients."

"We went inside, our weapons drawn, only to find the place was empty... save for the sorcerer. Sat at the center of the place, attempting to open some kind of portal to another dimension. We ordered him to stop, but he started casting fire spells everywhere. Not a good thing to be doing with flammable books everywhere."

"Leon battled him, as I attempted to control the flames. I managed to stop them, but as I turned to help my partner, he got struck with some spell and just... vanished. No sign of him, his armor or even his lucky dagger. He was just... gone."

"I got mad. I managed to knock the sorcerer out and drag him back to Overwatch. They threw him in a cell and I got my money... but Leon was nowhere to be found. We searched for weeks and months, but there wasn't a single trace of anything. He'd disappeared off the face of the earth, never to be seen again."

Rick sighed, staring off into the distance once again. I didn't dare speak.

"I never wanted to come back here. Too many bad memories. Still, don't really have a choice now. We've got a job to do, and by gum we're going to finish it, no matter what."

"I agree," I nodded, "and I'm sure that wherever Leon is now... he's proud of you."

"Heh, I doubt it," Rick grinned, "he hated Overwatch and the soldiers there. Probably thinks I'm a right idiot."

We both laughed, before marching off to get some sleep.

Day 10

The entry may say Day 10, and it's correct. However, it was VERY early in the day. Specifically, midnight.

We were all awoken to the screams of pain emerging from the depths of the museum. Rick, Steve, Amy, Viktor and I were all getting some sleep, while Winston and Boris patrolled for the intruder... who appeared to have been caught in one of our traps.

We raced to the room containing the blue power crystal. The floor was stained with lava and arrows had pierced the walls, but what had caught our thief was none other than the giant axe, which had trapped him by his underwear.

What did I tell you? Giant axes are unbeatable.

"NOOOOO!" Herobrine screamed, pounding his fist into the floor, "HOW COULD YOU FAIL? YOU WERE MY ONLY HOPE!"

I grinned. Looks like Herobrine wouldn't be coming back today. As Winston and Boris ran up to join us, Rick marched over to the thief. Dressed in leather armor dyed black and wearing a mask, it was clear he didn't want his identity revealed.

"Let's see who's really behind the mask."

Rick grasped the headgear and pulled off.

A silence befell the room, as our eyes fell upon the man who'd tried stealing the crystal. After a moment, I finally spoke up.

"Chad?"

Indeed it was him. There was no mistaking the rough-looking man who'd attempted to break into The Vault and who had aided us in tracking down the cult in the first place.

"I thought the cult had kidnapped you," said Rick, "what the heck are you doing here?"

Before he could give us an answer however, a low humming noise filled the air. Before I realized what was going on, the pedestal holding the crystal exploded, tossing us all across the room.

"IT WORKED!"

Oh no, not him again. I was practically begging for it not to be that particular person. But of course, it was none other than Red Robes.

"I can't believe it. I didn't think you'd all be stupid enough to fall for it… but it worked! You all played right into my hands, exactly as intended. And here I was worried you might actually work out what was going on. Haha, what a joke."

"What is he on about?" Steve demanded.

"I don't know, but I'll whack him with my stick if he doesn't shut up," Boris threatened, attempting to stand but failing.

"Don't you understand?" Red Robes asked, "I wanted you all here. I wanted you to come to the museum. I wanted you to stop Chad. That way, I could pull off my greatest trick ever!"

On his hand was Herobrine's Gauntlet, now glowing a mix of red and blue. Wait a second…

"Your plan has failed," I moaned, still feeling the pain from the explosion, "you just destroyed the blue crystal."

"You mean the fake you planted?" Red Robes giggled, "I already swapped the real one out with my own fake."

He showed me the gauntlet and to my sheer surprise and horror, there was indeed a blue crystal inserted into the weapon. Crud.

"YES! I LOVE THIS GUY!" Herobrine danced around in joy, "HE'S NOT AN IDIOT LIKE YOU LOT! OH WHY COULDN'T I GET STUCK WITH HIM!?"

CLANG!

As he'd been speaking, Rick had been reaching for his swords while playing dead. Waiting for the opportune moment to strike. The second Herobrine had started his dance routine, he'd leaped up and brought his swords down, intending on ending this whole farce once and for all. And it would have worked... if Red Robes hadn't grabbed his swords with the gauntlet.

"You don't even know the best part," the cultist chuckled as Rick struggled to free his blades, "the blue gem still has some extra juice left in it. Not enough to completely revive Herobrine... but just enough to transfer his spirit."

Before he could react, Red Robes wrenched the blades free from the Commander's hands and placed his hand on his head.

"RICK, NO!" I cried out, as the cultist began chanting.

Herobrine, lord of dark and shadow
Please hear my plea
Rise once more from the depths of eternal flames
And return again to wreak your terrible vengeance
Spare those who serve you, destroy those who oppose you
Oh great and powerful Herobrine, I beg of thee
Accept this sacrifice as a vessel
AND BE BORN ONCE MORE!

The last thing I saw was a brutal flash of light, before everything turned dark once more...

Book 6: Into the Nether Portal

Prologue

What have we unleashed?

If there's one thing Romero knows, its danger. I've seen things that could destroy the world a thousand times over. From ancient beings with untold power, to vast hordes of zombies, capable of munching their way through an entire city.

My experience with actual gods on the other hand... I'm a bit lacking there I'm afraid.

This is another diary, as you might have guessed. But not just any old diary. A diary that details what could be humanity's final battle. As I write this, I go forth with my companions to face a threat that could end all life everywhere. Which means that if you're reading this, one of two things has happened:

1. I won the battle and went on to become a very successful author.

2. You found this journal in some old ruins of a destroyed world.

Whatever the case is, you're in for the thrill ride of a lifetime. Out of the boiling cauldron and into the bottle as we say around my parts. One final battle that will truly decide the fate of the world…

Are you ready?

Day 1

"CHAMPIONS, STOP THEM!"

"Ah jeez mom, I don't want to go to school today," I moaned, my head throbbing.

It was around the time the ceiling exploded that I wasn't in my bed at home. Rather, I was lying on the cold, stone floor of Oldtown's museum. To the right, my blurry vision could make out Viktor attempting to swing his hammer at Chad the thief, who blocked it with his blade. To my left was Winston and Amy, firing knives and arrows at Red Robes, who deflected them with a simple spell.

And in front of me was Commander Rick- no, Herobrine, opening a gateway to what looked like a volcano.

"COMMANDER!" Boris ran forward with his stick, obviously aiming to bash Herobrine out of Rick's skull. The entity merely ducked, his eyes glowing a bright white, before knocking Boris away with a powerful kick. He then turned his attention back to the portal.

"ROMERO!"

I felt a hand help me to my feet, before passing me my blade.

"Thanks," I mumbled to Steve, who was drawing his own sword.

"Don't thank me yet, we've got work to do."

I nodded. Chad had just managed to knock Viktor's hammer away, but before he could deliver a finishing blow I opened a portal below him with my Blade of End. I figured an eternity spent with the Endermen and eating Endstone might do him some good.

I next planned on moving in to assist Winston and Amy, who were seemingly overwhelmed by Red Robes. But the cult leader spotted me, and with a grin (I'm guessing he was grinning under his hood), he called upon several skeleton servants.

"BEGONE!" Steve roared, smacking the husks of bone aside and moving in on R.R., who stepped away from his sword swing and blasted Steve with a fireball.

"Gah!" Steve clutched his arm, obviously hurt. Projectiles from Winston and Amy were keeping our foe on his toes, but no matter how quickly the knives and arrows arrived, each bounced off like it was nothing.

"Is that all you have?" he mocked, calling upon more skeletons.

"Try this on then," I shot back.

I swung my sword into the ground, a great surge of dark energy rising up from below. Red Robes tilted his head, as I directed the wave at him, tossing him through a display cabinet showing the bones of a Giant.

"Now for Rick," said Steve, to which I nodded in response.

But when we turned to face our friend-turned-foe, there was no one there. Only a tear in the fabric of space, showing a burning dimension…

Which was quickly closing.

"MOVE!" Steve yelled to the Champions, as we all made for the portal. Our only chance at getting Rick back.

"COME ON!" I cried, running as fast as my rotten legs would carry me. Only a few seconds left now…

We jumped…

And hit the stone wall behind the portal.

"Owwie."

Day 2

I gotta say, that was a pretty good escape on Herobrine's part. And I'm not one for complimenting people.

We just missed the portal, instead hitting the wall behind it. Unfortunately, such a blow managed to knock the lot of us out, allowing Red Robes to make his escape as well. Which left us in the Overworld, with no clues as to where Rick or Red Robes were and with no idea on how to get to them.

We're also out of chips and dip, making this situation ever direr.

Fortunately, I am the master of good luck. As proven here.

As it turns out, the Curator himself knows a bit more about Herobrine than he lets on. When he wasn't willing to talk, we had to use extreme interrogation techniques.

"Stop, please!" he cried out in laughter, as Viktor used several feathers to extract the information.

"ALRIGHT, I'LL TELL YOU!"

According to the Curator, the place where Herobrine now resides is a dimension that was thought to exist only in legend. The Nether. A fiery landscape, fraught with peril and inhabited by the most dangerous of all monsters. Said to be created during the time when Herobrine had his own body, its home to everything he'll need to destroy Minecraftia.

Sigh. Why do all the villains want to destroy the planet? Gets kind of boring after a while.

The question here of course is how we actually get to the Nether. Well, our good friend the Curator has the answer once again!

They had this thing in storage, apparently planning on making it an exhibit. Of course, opening a portal to Herobrine's home isn't the best tourist attraction. Ah well.

Once we've gathered some supplies, we'll activate the portal and head on through. There, we'll find a way to save Rick and defeat Herobrine… or despawn in the process.

Day 3

The operation begins!

We've sourced everything we need for the upcoming assault on Herobrine's homeworld. First and most importantly: bottled water. Water will actually evaporate in seconds due to the intense heat in the Nether, so we'll have to bring plenty if we're going to stay hydrated. Food is a necessity of course, but the Curator tells me mushrooms grow in the Nether as well.

We've also upgraded our armor with heat resistance, just to help us handle the temperatures. Finally, we're well-stocked on arrows, as the Curator has oh-so wisely informed me of the airborne creatures which reside in the Nether. Ghasts. They're known for being massive, difficult to defeat and for shooting fireballs. Fun.

To activate the portal, we need to use Flint 'n Steel to… light it up I guess? That's the only known method for humans to travel to the Nether, according to the *'How to travel to the Nether Handbook'* the Curator was kind enough to lend us.

I elected we head to the Nether today, but Steve refused. According to him, we need to rest up and recover from our last battle before we can head into that accursed dimension. If you ask me, we can't afford to waste any more time. Who knows what Herobrine is doing with Rick? He could be making him complete dangerous tasks, construct giant statues in his image or... or...

He could be forcing him to dance for his amusement!!!

We move tomorrow. We're getting Rick back, no matter what.

Day 4

The Nether. The final frontier.

We made our way into the storage room, where we found the hulking pile of Obsidian waiting for us. Steve and I were equipped with the Flint 'n Steel, while the others were lugging large crates with our vital supplies.

"Once you arrive in the Nether, another portal will be created in the spot you land," the Curator explained, "I doubt you'll find any other portals there, so make sure you use this one to get back. On the off chance that you do find another gateway, don't take it."

"Why not?" Winston raised an eyebrow.

"A scientist once calculated that every step you take in the Nether is the equivalent to taking eight steps in the Overworld. If you take a different portal back to the Overworld, who knows where you'll end up?"

"Roger that, we'll try to avoid it," Steve nodded, before the pair of us approached the portal. Taking a deep breath, we lit the Obsidian.

The purple gateway opened immediately, and dark voices began to spew out. Whispers and strange noises, hinting at something dark and terrible lurking behind it.

"Ignore it," the Curator ordered, "it's nothing to be afraid of. Only the souls of those who got lost in the portal, never to return."

How very reassuring. With those wonderful thoughts in mind, we approached the portal, ready to enter the twisted dimension.

"And one last thing!" the Curator cried out, as we were inches from the portal.

I turned, and noticed that for perhaps the first time, the old man had a smile on his face.

"Good luck," he whispered.

And so, I stepped into the living, burning nightmare…

Let me tell you that travelling between dimensions really makes you feel ill.

Ugh, the second I stepped out of that portal I wanted to spew everywhere. However, I was somewhat distracted by the environment around me. Purple stone, forming the floor, walls and ceiling like dirt and cobble. Fiery falls of lava, descending from the very roof of the world. In the distance, I could hear a pig squealing. A few moments later, Steve stepped out from behind me, equally as impressed.

This was indeed the Nether, in all of its glory. Everything that had been said about this world was true. The blazing landscape, the evil feel, the giant white monster floating towards us.

Oh crud.

Fireballs descended on us almost immediately, as the Ghast let out a horrific cry of anger. Steve and I leaped left and right, as the charge flew past us…

And into the portal.

The purple gateway disappeared, leaving a blank, empty frame. Our only way out of the Nether had just been destroyed.

"MOVE ROMERO!" Steve cried, pushing me back to my senses.

The pair of us ran, as the Ghast continued to rain down destruction above us. The fireballs launched by the creature tore apart the environment, blasting the ground to smithereens and setting it alight. It was all we could do to run for our very lives, attempting to reach some form of shelter.

After what seemed like an eternity, I spotted it. A small cave buried into the wall, only a short distance away.

"Go for it," I told Steve, "I'll draw this thing's attacks."

Steve nodded, dashing on ahead as I taunted and waved at the Ghast.

"Come and get me," I shook my rear-end at the beast, which seemed to anger it quite a bit. Half a dozen more fireballs flew towards me, and I dived for the nearest portion of cover, which was promptly blown to bits.

"HURRY ROMERO!" Steve yelled, having made it to the cave entrance.

Figuring I'd annoyed the Ghast enough for one day, I sprinted away as fast as I could manage. Explosions seemed to follow me like a disgusting smell, but I outran them all, eventually making it to the safety of the cave.

"Nice one," Steve grinned, as I sat down to catch my breath. What a chase that had been.

"What now?" I wheezed to my companion, before the reality of the situation dawned on me.

We were trapped. The portal was damaged, and the majority of our allies and supplies were on the other side of it. Steve however, merely shrugged.

"We go onwards," he said, "we find Rick, get Herobrine out of his body and then get that ghost to send us home. Whatever it takes."

I nodded. Whatever it takes.

Day 5

"Wakey, wakey, sleeping beauty!"

I rose, rubbing my eyes with one hand and drawing my sword with the other.

"Now that's not a way to treat your guests, is it?"

Steve was pinned to the floor, a blocky foot on his chest. The man standing on him was none other than Rick, with white glowing eyes.

"Release him!" I demanded, pointing the Blade of Ender at the Rick/Herobrine entity, "Or I will destroy you."

"Not a problem," Rickbrine grinned, "just bring me the third power stone and I'll gladly return your friend."

Wait, what?

Rickbrine flashed the gauntlet, containing the red and blue stones, "I snatched this off of the cultist before we got separated. I came back to this accursed place, thinking I could retrieve the third stone… I didn't realize how dangerous it was for a mortal."

"What's the matter? Can't handle the heat?" I joked.

Somewhere, I could hear an audience groaning.

"Not funny," Steve croaked. Herobrine however, chuckled.

"Minecraftians are so weak. No matter, I have you two now."

Wait, what?

"I need the pair of you to journey into my temple and secure the final power stone. Bring it back to me, and not only shall I release your friend Rick, but I will also provide safe passage home. I understand that your only working portal was damaged."

I gritted my teeth. So he'd been following us.

"Judging from your supplies, you don't exactly have a lot of time either, so I'd hurry up and make a decision if I were you. Not that there's a decision to make. I'm offering you a way out and if you don't take it, I'll just wait for your other friends to show up and –"

Rickbrine froze, clutching his head in pain. He fell down on one knee, groaning.

"Not again," he moaned, "why can't you stay down?"

That voice. That wasn't Herobrine's echoing tones. That was...

"Romero! Steve!" Rick cried out, struggling to stand, "You mustn't help him! You have no idea what he's planning to! You must-"

Rick moaned in pain, collapsing once more. When he rose, we were speaking to Herobrine, not our friend.

"He still resists," Herobrine noted, "I admire him for that. But it's foolish."

"What are you planning?" Steve coughed, clambering to his feet.

"You'll see soon enough," Rickbrine grinned, "now I suggest you head for the temple and get the stone. Once you're done, meet me on the bridge leading to the temple. I'll release your friend and give you a free ride home."

"And how can we trust you?" I questioned.

Rickbrine only shrugged.

"You can't," he said simply, "and that's the fun of it. I give you three days till you run out of supplies, so get to work chaps. I'll see you soon!"

And with a snap of his fingers, he was gone, leaving us with a difficult choice ahead.

Day 6

Two paths, each with nasty results.

If we help Rickbrine, then we have to venture into his temple. We'll be forced to confront all sorts of evil creatures, avoid all manner of traps and have to apply sunblock every few minutes. Assuming we make it through all of that, we then need to acquire the green power crystal and return it to Rickbrine, whereupon he will use its power to regain his old body.

Assuming he's totally trustworthy (and believe me when I say he isn't), he'll hold up his end of the bargain by returning Rick to us, safe and sound, before resurrecting his old body and possibly invading Minecraft. Unless he's nice enough to stick around this awful place, which I'm pretty sure he isn't. On the bright side, he might give us front row tickets to watch the destruction of the world.

On the other hand, if we turn down Rickbrine's offer then we're left trapped in this awful place, left to burn and with no possibility of escape. Even if we do manage to make it back to the Overworld, Herobrine still has Rick. Chances are he'll probably use him to get the green power crystal anyway. And if he does succeed, Rick is finished.

So we're going to have to come up with a third option. Find a way to obtain the power crystal and to free Rick, without resurrecting Herobrine. A lot tougher than it looks by the way.

For now, we're on our way to Herobrine's temple. We're going to try and get this crystal, all while coming up with another crafty scheme. Or rather, I will. Steve isn't the craftiest person around.

"I can hear you y'know!"

Whatever. We've got two days of supplies remaining. I suppose we'd better make this quick.

Day 7

Eh, my place is bigger.

Our journey here wasn't the easiest. We managed to avoid the Ghasts roaming this place last night, but soon found ourselves encounter a new foe. Zombie Pigmen.

Strangely enough, they don't actually attack you. Not at first. They seem quite... docile. I can only assume that the tasty pig that makes up 50% of these zombies keeps them calm. In fact, you only really run into trouble when you accidentally hit one of them.

As Steve did, when a Pigman frightened him.

He'd only struck one, but half a dozen of them converged on our position, attempting to cut us to pieces. We fought back of course, managing to drive the creatures away, but not without sustaining a few injuries.

And now we're here. Herobrine's Temple. Already I'm fearing what we're going to encounter. If Ghasts and Zombie Pigmen are for starters, I can only imagine what

Herobrine is offering up for the main course.

"Well done on making it this far," Rickbrine clapped, leaning on some kind of Netherbrick, "the temple is up ahead. I wouldn't linger too long on the bridge, seeing as Ghasts like to float on by here. Once you're inside, make your way to the treasure room at the bottom of the fortress."

"What can you tell us about the monsters?" I asked.

"That temple was constructed to guard my most precious artefacts," Rickbrine grinned, "so it has some pretty decent security. Blazes, humans I transformed into fiery monsters, can be found floating about the place. Watch out for them, seeing as they shoot fireballs fairly quickly."

Great.

"What else?"

"On the lower levels, you'll probably run into some Magma Cubes. They're like slimes, only much nastier. If they swallow you up, they'll probably burn you to cinders."

Fantastic.

"Anything else?"

"Only one last thing. Keep an eye out for the warrior that guards the treasure room."

"What kind of warrior?" Steve asked.

"One of my experiments gone wrong. Or gone right, depending on how you look at it. His strength is beyond anything you've ever seen, so I'd try and avoid him."

"What a lovely day this is turning out to be," Steve sighed, "any advice for the traps?"

"Don't trigger them," Rickbrine chuckled, "good luck you two. See you here in a couple of days."

A couple of days. Could we last that long? The heat was really starting to get to me, judging from the sweat on my leather armor. Steve didn't look much better. Give Rick a wave, the pair of us began to cross the bridge.

True to Herobrine's word, Ghasts did indeed start firing on us. We decided to pick up the pace and race for the entrance, a small arch with an open gate. Explosions sounded behind us like cannon fire, but we paid it no heed and instead dashed inside.

The interior was a sight to behold. A vast ceiling and a spacious floor. Strange plants grew to the left and right, and a short distance away sat a massive throne. As much as I would have loved to sit in it, we had no time to rest. We instead focused our sights on the staircase, labeled 'Treasure Room this way. NO THIEVES ALLOWED!'

The descent took us to a room built into the side of the mountain. Windows overlooked an ocean of lava, and a bridge connected this part of the fortress with another. There were no other routes leading out of the room.

"Guess we have to cross," I said to Steve.

Before we could leave the room however, a click rung in our eyes. We looked to our feet, spotting a pressure plate the same color as the floor. What followed were deep, wheezy groans, and the sound of a burning fire.

We turned, only to be greeted with Herobrine's creations. Blazes.

I glanced to Steve, who'd already pulled out a bow and begun firing. One went down in a couple of shots, but the others took no heed, instead electing to blast us with a fire attack. We took this as our cue to run like heck.

"Herobrine couldn't have invented unicorns, could he?" I shouted to Steve, who smiled and shook his head.

"Nah, but this makes it a whole lot more fun."

And with that statement, he turned and fired off a few more arrows, taking down a pair of Blazes. He'd been practicing, it would seem. At any rate, my stumpy zombie hands weren't really fit for shooting bows. So I threw my spare sword at them.

"BULLSEYE!" I grinned, as the creature disappeared in a cloud of smoke. Steve however raised an eyebrow, as the sword toppled into the lava below.

"Well crud," I sighed, and we both continued on our way, my companion pausing to shoot any Blaze which drew too close.

When we finally reached the other side, I flipped a switch built into the wall. The gate hovering above the room came crashing down, preventing the burning creatures from entering. We were safe, albeit exhausted.

"We should rest," Steve recommended, "we're running low on steam and we've got a ways to go yet."

I agreed, resting against the wall as I shut my eyes, the worries in my mind leaving me as I slept.

Day 8

I awoke to a dry mouth and a headache.

Steve didn't look much better than I did, as he rubbed his eyes and reached for a vial of water. One of the two we had left. He poured half of it down his throat before handing me the remainder, which I gulped up eagerly.

"We'd better hurry and find that darned power crystal," Steve muttered, coughing slightly. The Nether was no place for a mortal to live.

And so, groaning, we rose to our feet and climbed down the staircase, taking us deeper into the fortress.

"Do you have any ideas?" Steve asked, after a short time.

"Ideas?"

"Yeah, like how do we defeat Herobrine without giving him the crystal?"

"No clue," I admitted, "and normally I'm good with ideas."

"Well you'd better put that big brain of yours to work. We're running out of time."

I nodded, deciding to save my scratchy voice till I needed it most.

The descent must have taken fifteen minutes at the very least, and that was tiring enough. I was dreading having to return that way. After some time, I began hearing bubbling noises above us. Liquid. It soon occurred to me we were below the lava oceans of the Nether.

Steve must have had the same thought: "We're pretty deep now. Certainly a good place for Herobrine to hide his treasure."

Finally, we emerged in a small, underground chamber. A short distance away sat an iron door with a button, which would hopefully take us to our prize. It was what was in front of us however that caught my attention.

"Must be the Magma Cube that Herobrine mentioned," I whispered to Steve.

"Either way, it's finished," he grinned, pulling back on his bow string and letting loose an arrow.

It only hit me at that moment that these were the Nether variants of Slimes, which meant...

The Magma Cube split into two smaller, yet equally as dangerous cubes. Not too happy with being shot at, they moved in on us.

"FOR RICK!" Steve cried, taking his sword in

favor of his bow and cutting the nearest monster into chunks. I did the same.

Despawn one, and two more would appear. It didn't seem to matter how many we actually cut down, they just kept splitting into smaller and smaller variants. They grew closer and closer, the heat coming off them enough to burn my leather armor.

"Think of something!" Steve cried, as one of the cubes jumped on his arm.

It was all I could do to keep slashing, solutions whizzing through my head. I decided to choose the one which made the most sense. The most dangerous one for that matter.

I reached into Steve's backpack and pulled out a vial of water, which I threw at the horde of cubes. It promptly shattered, dousing the majority of the creatures in the liquid. I don't know if it was some allergic reaction, some dislike of water or some form of luck, because they immediately began to melt.

"Let's go," I tugged Steve onwards towards the door, hitting the button and continuing onwards to our destination.

"Err... Romero?"

"What?" I turned around, noticing my companion staring at the wall... and the lack of a button.

I groaned. Iron doors were too heavy to open

normally. You needed a button, a lever or a pressure plate. And we were lacking in all three.

"Another trap," I sighed, "whatever, let's just keep going."

And so, the two brave companions ventured on, continuing down the path that would lead them to the mystical object of power sought after by Herobrine. They –

"That's enough Romero," Steve sighed, as we reached the final room.

There wasn't much remarkable about this place. Just a few Netherbrick walls, a statue of a black skeleton wielding a sword, and a pedestal…

Holding the green power crystal.

"There it is," Steve grinned, racing over to grab it. But as he did, a clicking noise caught my attention, as did the twitching of the "statue".

"STEVE, LOOK OUT!" I cried, pushing him to the floor as the skeleton swung its blade, cracking the wall behind us.

We scrambled to our feet, as the skeleton retrieved its blade and marched towards us. This had to be the warrior Herobrine told us about. The one with untold strength. Like things hadn't been difficult enough.

"FOR MINECRAFT!" Steve parried an attack from the monster and swung at its legs, only for the skeleton to deflect the attack and follow up with a stab to Steve's side.

My companion jumped back, and I stepped in, pushing the sword back and aiming to cut off its arm.

It ended up catching my blade with its hand.

"Just what kind of monster is this?" I asked myself, as the creature crushed the sharpness of my sword in its hands.

That was immediately followed by an explosion.

I was tossed into the wall like a doll, holding the now useless hilt of my sword. Steve was up on his feet, battling the monster with one hand while grabbing the power crystal with the other.

"RUN!" Steve called to me, but I paid him no heed.

The Blade of End. The most powerful sword ever forged by humans. Created to defeat the Ender Dragon itself. A trusty weapon which had served me for years, destroyed in an instant. Just what were we up against?

"MOVE!"

I was pulled back to the present, the skeleton looming over me. I jumped backwards, into the cramped hallway which had led us to this point. In front of us was the locked iron door. Behind us was the invincible skeleton.

We were trapped.

Epilogue

"How much longer?" Boris asked, as Winston pounded away on the portal with his pickaxe.

"Just a bit longer," the champion muttered, "pass me a shovel."

"Are we certain they're still alive?" Amy asked, tossing Winston the tool, "it's been days, Winston."

"We can't give up. And even if they have been despawned, we need to save Rick and stop Herobrine."

"That won't be happening," a voice chuckled behind them.

The three champions turned, finding themselves face-to-face with, as Romero had put it, Red Robes.

"Champions, prepare for battle!" Winston announced, drawing his knives. Amy equipped her bow and Boris took hold of his stick.

"There's no need for such violence," said Red Robes, shaking his head, "after all, defeating me won't stop

Herobrine."

"He's next on the list," Amy quipped, "now how about you surrender before we kick your butt?"

"I'm afraid not my dear," Red Robes shook his head, instead electing to remove his hood, "for if anyone will be surrendering, it will be you three."

Winston smirked, preparing to toss one of his knives… but he felt hesitant. Reluctant even. The man didn't look any different to the other Minecraftians he'd fought, so what was stopping him? Was it his calm gaze? His smile?

Or was it his piercing red eyes, which seemed to stare into his very soul?

"You will serve only one. Herobrine. And here, I give to you your mission. Enter the Nether, find the ones you call Romero and Steve and strike them down."

Book 7: The Lost Comrades

Prologue

Okay chaps, this is another message from your pal Romero.

If you're reading this, then chances are I've been defeated and Herobrine has risen once again. If that's the case, then first allow me to apologize for all the trouble he's probably causing right now. Knowing him, he's probably set fire to a stack of logs and laughed about it non-stop for the past few hours.

Still, there's also a chance we've managed to defeat him. If that's instead the case but there is still some maniac running amok, setting fire to logs, I highly recommend you call the Admins as quickly as you can. You may also want to move all wood inside.

At any rate, this is just another chapter in the

extraordinary tale of Rick, Romero, Steve and Herobrine, in an epic quest to save the world and defeat the forces of evil. If they end up making a movie about us, that's just a bonus.

Steel yourself reader, for this is the most epic installment in the series yet. The tale of Romero and Steve facing fallen gods and crazy cult leaders. All in a days work for the heroes of Minecraftia.

Sit back and enjoy.

Day 1

We last left our heroes in the very jaws of danger, facing down the most powerful of Herobrine's creation. Would they escape by the skin of their teeth? Or would they join countless others in the inferno of the –

"FOR THE LOVE OF NOTCH, COULD YOU STOP ACTING LIKE THIS IS A MOVIE?"

Sorry Steve!

The Wither Skeleton had us trapped between a rock and a hard place. Behind us was an iron door, too heavy to be opened by our scrawny hands. In front of us was the skeleton of course, who looked ready to slice us into pork chops. The creature held its black sword above its head, ready to strike us down in one, fell swoop.

"Got any ideas?" Steve asked, as the blade descended.

"Just one," I grinned, "DODGE!"

I stepped left and Steve hop to the right, as the blade crashed down, missing its target and instead ripping apart the iron door behind us. The skeleton paused, its weapon trapped with the ruins of the door. This was our chance.

"NOW!"

Steve dived forward, twirling and spinning his sword, before slicing it through the neck of the skeleton. The skull was propelled several blocks, and the creature's body soon turned to bone meal.

"Nice one," I remarked. Steve did deserve the odd compliment here and there...

"ALL HAIL STEVE! THE GREATEST WARRIOR WHO EVER LIVED!"

Just as long as they don't make his head any bigger.

***

We fled from the treasure room, through the various areas we'd passed on our journey here, up several flights of stairs and, on one occasion, had to climb a ladder. A LADDER! As if things had not been exhausting enough already. I could barely drag myself to the top, the lack of water really taking a toll on my zombie organs.

Steve seemed to be just fine, sporting nonsense about he was the most powerful hero in the history of Minecraftia and that when we got back, they were going to construct a statue in his honor.

"Because after all, I am the slayer of Herobrine's most powerful creation. There is no foe who can hope to match me on the battlefield!"

"Lava might cause you a bit of trouble," I noted.

"Even lava fears to flow near me," he grinned.

"True, but what if someone was to push you into a pit of it?"

That shut him up.

At long last, we arrived at our destination. The bridge leading to Herobrine's Temple. Fortunately, there were no Ghasts in sight. Across the path of Netherbrick sat Rickbrine, messing with some kind of gaming device in his hand.

"STUPID PIXELMON!" he snarled, tossing the console into the lava below, "I so should have caught that guy. Oh hey, you guys are back. How was the temple? Have a nice time?"

"It was wonderful," I spat, "I'll be sure to come back next year."

"Sweet," Rickbrine grinned, "but the question remains... did you guys manage to succeed in your mission?"

I glanced at Steve with solemn eyes, and he seemed to share my expression. If we gave Herobrine the last power crystal, he'd be at full strength and ready to take over the Overworld. I'd only had a taste of what his minions were capable of. A whole army of Blazes, Magma Cubes and Ghasts would put an end to life as we knew it.

With a sigh, I reached into my pocket, searching for

the object. My fingers brushed over it, and with a deep breath, I removed it and presented the green gem to Herobrine.

"Excellent," he chuckled, "oh this is wonderful."

Without a moment's hesitation, as if expecting me to snatch it back, Herobrine took the object and fitted it into his gauntlet. Red, blue and green now lit up his weapon like a discount rainbow. He took a few seconds to admire his new collection, before giving us a beaming smile.

"Oh well done Romero! Well done Steve! You two defied the odds and brought me the object I so desired. Of course, I am a man of my word. Therefore, I shall return not only Rick's body, but I shall also grant you safe passage back to the Overworld. Of course, if you want to stick around for my resurrection, then that would be fine."

"Wouldn't miss it for the world," Steve said calmly.

"Wonderful!"

With a snap of his fingers, a bright flash illuminated the already bright Nether. A pulsing glow that threatened to blind both Steve and I. When it faded, Rick was bending on one knee, panting heavily. Above him floated a ghostly entity, grinning with glee.

"My resurrection is at hand," Herobrine proclaimed, as a black tear in the world opened behind us. The portal home. Any second now, we'd be making a dash for it…

"Watch and tremble in fear mortals, as life as you

know it slowly comes to an end. I, the great and powerful Herobrine, shall bring about the end of this world and all worlds. You shall all bare witness to my return, and you shall gaze upon the destruction of Minecraftia by my hand. You shall have front row seats to the fires that shall wipe the world clean and remake it in my image. You shall-"

"Hey, Herojerk!" I called out "You might want to take another look at your power crystal."

He glared at me for a few seconds, first out of confusion, then out of worry. His eyes grew wide and his mouth dropped open. He raised the gauntlet to his face, examining the gems within. The red power crystal, the blue power crystal…

And the green emerald. Exactly the same as any old emerald you could use to trade with. Worth quite a bit of money, but absolutely nothing in evil magic.

"YOU TRICKED ME!" Herobrine roared, "YOU DARE TO FOOL THE GREAT AND MIGHTY HEROBRINE!?"

"Nice work," Rick coughed, clambering to his feet, "now let's get out of here."

"YOU WON'T LEAVE, I WON'T ALLOW IT!" Herobrine declared, speeding towards me and swinging his fist, which passed harmlessly through my body.

"Looks like your luck has run out," I chuckled, and Herobrine screamed in anger.

"MINIONS, DESTORY THEM!" he barked, waving his hand.

It was as if the sky itself had torn open. Above us, dozens of Ghasts and Blazes descended from Herobrine's fortress, blasting fireballs in our direction. Steve paused to snipe a couple of them, but we did not outstay our welcome.

"STOP THEM!"

Explosions battered the ground left and right, but none managed to find their mark. And although Herobrine was desperately trying to shut the portal as fast as he could, it wasn't fast enough. We raced across the burning round with phenomenal speed, and dived through the gateway back to our realm.

"NOOOOOOOOOOOOOOOOOOOOOOO!"

***

We'd done it.

We'd been to the Nether and survived.

So where's my medal?

Nah, just kidding.

We were back in the museum. More precisely, in the exhibit of the blue power crystal. It didn't look much different to how we'd left it before. Broken glass and scorch marks stained the ground, showcasing the battle which had taken place here oh so recently.

"I can't believe that actually worked," Steve breathed.

"Of course it worked, it was my idea," I shrugged.

Rick and Steve glanced at each other, as if to say "that totally wasn't his idea". Pfft. Details, details.

"The museum's awfully empty," I remarked, glancing around the empty chamber. Just where was everyone?

"Strange…" Steve noted, as we began to explore the seemingly empty museum.

And there was truly no one in sight. We investigated a variety of the exhibits, from the history of Notch's beard to the strange and peculiar smell of slimes. Yet our investigations yielded nothing. It was as if everyone in the museum had disappeared.

"They must be back at our room," Rick decided, to which we agreed.

Still, all that matters is that we're back in the Overworld, and that there's nothing else to worry about!

"Ahem."

We turned.

"Oh dear"

Nothing to worry about except for our friends, now sporting glowing purpling eyes and pointing their weapons at us.

Day 2

Well, this is a fine mess we've gotten ourselves into.

It seems to me that recently, all we've managed to do is get ourselves captured. In fact, my whole life has been about getting thrown in a darned cell. Back when Rick and I were enemies I got locked up in Overwatch. After that I got thrown into a cell by the Cult of Herobrine. And now, I've been locked up by my closest friends.

Oh yeah, there was plenty of times were I got captured and locked up in between all of those other instances, but those are just the most important and most memorable.

So my friends weren't exactly happy to see us. I mean, I know they're being controlled by some other entity, but they were pretty angry.

"We spent the last twelve hours searching for you morons in the Nether!" Winston hissed.

"Do you have any idea how hot it is in there?" Amy demanded.

Oh believe me, we do.

We've got no idea what's happened to them, nor how we can reverse it. It's obvious they've been possessed, but we're still working on a solution to de-possess them. Of course, that solution means we have to bust out of here somehow. Which is kind of difficult. Allow me to show you why.

They didn't just throw us in any old prison, which wouldn't be a problem to escape from. I'm an old pro at this now. Oh no, they had to find the darkest, most secure prison in the entire server. None other than Blocktraz...

Okay, that's not a real thing but it might as well be.

This entire compound isn't all that big. Just a few hundred blocks or so. They make up for that with iron bars, iron doors, iron walls and even iron golems. You can bet that if anything iron exists, they've got it here.

Escaping won't be easy, but we'll figure something out. In the meantime, we have to figure out who's behind these possessions. Which shouldn't be too difficult, seeing as there's like two bad guys in this whole story.

"Story?" asked Steve.

NEVERMIND! I said nothing. Ahem. What I meant is that they're aren't many suspects. And knowing how bad guys act in this story-

"What's this about a story?" Rick asked.

266

Never you mind Rick! As I was saying, knowing how the baddies have been acting so far, I think it's fairly safe to say that they'll visit us to gloat about their victory and about how there's nothing we can do to stop their plans. And knowing how the story goes-

"Why do you keep talking about a story?"

I SAID NOTHING!

At any rate, expect a visit tomorrow.

Day 3

I should have bet money on the bad guy visiting us.

"I don't understand how you managed to make such a lucky guess," said Rick, scratching his head.

Oh if only he knew.

Ladies and gentlemen, Steves and Alexes, our bad guy is none other than the notorious cult leader. Please, put your blocky hands together for the one, the only, Red Robes!

"I have a name you know," he sighed as he limped through the door.

"Oh yeah? And what is it?" I asked.

"Like I'd tell you," he rolled his eyes, "now, I bet you're wondering what's going on her-"

"You possessed our friends with your crazy magical powers and locked us up here so we couldn't stop whatever your planning," Rick sighed, "Do you take me for an idiot?"

"How did you figure out my amazing plan?" Red Robes cried, collapsing to his knees.

We really need some better bad guys.

"If you must know, then yes, I am the one who possessed the other Champions and bent them to my will. I'm also responsible for locking you up here so that you can't interfere with my plans."

"Why not possess us like the rest?" Steve demanded, a look of horror passing over both my face and Rick's. That guy could be a real idiot at times.

"Slight problem with that," Red Robes pointed out, "Magic in Minecraft is a very delicate and strange art. Even the most powerful magicians don't understand it. For reasons unknown to all, a person can only be possessed by magic ONCE."

Now THAT was interesting. Mr. Troll had previously possessed Steve, and Rick had just escaped the clutches of Herobrine's mind hug. The pair of them couldn't be controlled, it would seem.

But wait, I hadn't been possessed by anything. Which meant...

"Don't worry Romero, I haven't forgotten about you," Red Robes grinned, "your mind should be easy to control. And once I have your intelligence, there's not a thing anyone do to stop me."

Red Robes pulled down his hood, and my

companions were forced to look away as a blinding flash of red filled the room.

"You are now my servant, Romero the Zombie," hissed the demonic voice of Red Robes, "from this day until the end of days, you shall answer my beck and call. My every order will be yours to obey, and you shall never refuse me."

"You might want to look again," I quipped.

Red Robes dimmed down his laser vision, glaring as he spotted the mirror glued to my face.

"My emergency mirror," I grinned, "never leave home without it."

"Curses," Red Robes spat, "I can't possess him with that mirror on his face, and if I break it I'll get seven years' worth of bad luck."

"Lose lose, no matter what you choose," I chuckled.

"Bah," Red Robes ran a hand down his red robes, "you may have won this time Romero, but you won't always have that mirror to protect you. And when the day comes that you are weak and unsuspecting, then I shall strike you down like the vermin you are."

And with that, he left the room, his presence remaining in the air like… like a fart.

"So what now?" asked Rick.

"We need to find a way out of here," I replied,

"before he completes whatever evil deeds he's plotting."

And find a way out we would.

Day 4

We have a plan!

This is truly one of the worst prisons imaginable. Well, bad for us at any rate. It's the perfect combination of the best security systems known in Minecraft. One mistake, one fault, and we'd be despawned faster than we could blink.

Aside from the tough walls, bars and doors, the Iron Golems that roam outside our cells are known to destroy any intruder who happens to attempt an escape. We saw this with another pair of people stationed here, who managed to get past the door and soon found themselves mushed against the wall.

But there is one story in Minecraft which many have come to hear. The story of the relationship between the Iron Golems and the Testificates, the villagers of the world. The legends tell of how the Iron Golems would protect the villages and the inhabitants from zombies, skeletons and other evil creatures. In times of peace, the Golems would even give roses to the people of the village.

"THIS STILL DOESN'T EXPLAIN WHY I HAVE TO DRESS UP LIKE A FILTHY VILLAGER!"

Jeez Steve, someone woke up on the wrong side of the bed.

"THAT'S BECAUSE THE BED IS MADE OF OBISIDIAN BLOCKS!"

Yeah, they should really fix that.

Using our blankets, a few sets of cocoa beans we managed to smuggle in and a stuffed pillow, we managed to dress Steve up to look like a villager.

It looked perfect! But would it be enough to get us past the Iron Golems?

"HELP! HELP!" I cried, as Steve lay down on the floor.

Immediately, a pair of Golems burst through the door, searching for signs of disturbance. They entered to find myself and Rick panicking over poor Villager Steve, who was lying on the floor, clutching his stomach.

"You must help us!" I begged the Golems, "the poor villager just collapsed. We've got no idea what's wrong with him! Please, you must help the poor Testificate."

The Golems glanced at each other. Although incapable of human speech, they seemed to understand. They nudged Steve a few times with their feet, before bending down to get a closer look.

"NOW!" I yelled.

Steve sprang up, sticking a pillowcase over one of the Golems' head. I struck the other myself, with a block of Obsidian taken from my bed frame.

"How'd you like that?" I sneered at the Iron giant.

I swear to Notch, the Golem shrugged it off like it was nothing and punched me into the wall. I of course, took it like a champ.

"You cried and moaned for twenty minutes, after he gently tapped you over the head."

SILENCE!

The details aren't important. What mattered was that we managed to subdue the Iron Golems and steal the keys to the cells from them. Now, we could have left there and then, in an attempt to track down Red Robes before he finished whatever evil plans he was coming up with.

There was just the small matter of dealing with the possessed Boris.

"None shall pass!" he declared, spinning his large stick and pointing it at us. The Stick of Hitting. Boris' trademark weapon. Crafted from the finest trees in Minecraftia, he had given many a foe a headache with this particular baton. Defeating him would be no easy feat.

"YAAAAAAAAAAH!"

Rick leapt through the air, block of Obsidian in

hand. Boris looked upwards, his eyes widening, as the Commander brought Minecraft's second strongest block down upon his head.

"Oh my brain cells," Boris moaned, stumbling back and forth, "wait, where am I?"

"You can't fool me Red Robes," Rick declared, striking Boris again in a comedic fashion, "I know you've still possessed Boris. Give him back to us!"

"What?" Boris spluttered, as the cube struck him again, "OUCH! Dude, what the heck? It's me! Boris!"

"Do you take me for an idiot?"

"Yes!"

WHACK!

"OUCH!"

This process went on for several minutes, with Rick attempting to beat Red Robe's influence out of the poor guy. Of course, Steve and I had already figured out Boris was back to normal.

"Okay, I'm pretty sure he's back to normal," I finally said, walking up to Rick, who stood over an unconscious Boris.

"Why yes mother, I would like to hit them with a stick," he mumbled in his sleep.

"STOP INTRUDERS!"

Arrows flew down to our position, as Winston and Amy closed in with another dozen Iron Golems. We had long outstayed our welcome. It was time to get the fudge out of dodge.

"Let's go!" I shouted to Steve and Rick, the latter throwing Boris over his shoulder. We ran for the exit, our former companions in hot pursuit.

"I'll buy us a little bit of time," Steve said, "toss me the keys!"

I did so, and the Champion began running up to the cells. A few seconds later, he'd opened a dozen doors, releasing some of the most dangerous criminals in Minecraft history. From Mr. TNT to The Jester, these were among the nastiest players to ever walk the server.

Which is why we released them to use as bait.

"GET 'EM LADS!" Muscle Maniac roared, a single punch reverting an Iron Golem to its original, iron block form.

"Wanna hear a joke?" The Jester giggled, throwing a pie in Winston's face.

We took this as our cue to leave.

With the keys, we managed to escape the prison (after releasing a few more prisoners) and make it to the nearby city of Blocktopia. I know, these names really aren't original for a game-

"A game?" Rick questioned.

I mean, a world made up of blocks. Still, we were able to nab a nice little apartment for the night, letting us rest up.

"So what's the next move?" I asked Rick, shortly before hitting the sack.

"We need to rescue the others," Rick replied, "then we can take the fight to Red Robes. Once he's eliminated, we won't have to worry anymore. Herobrine's been defeated, and Red Robes doesn't have his cultist army anymore. Once we have the guys back, he'll have nowhere else to run."

The plan sounds good, but from what I've seen previously, there's bound to be something that's gonna go wrong.

Day 5

"Wakey, wakey, sleeping beauty!"

I rose, rubbing my eyes with one hand and drawing my sword with the other. Last time I'd heard those words, Rickbrine had been grinning at me.

And lo and behold, Rick was standing at the other end of the room, a cup of boiling liquid in one hand and a sword in the other.

"Don't tell me Herobrine got you again," I sighed, not really feeling up to a battle this second.

"What are you talking about?" he asked, raising an eyebrow, "I just wanted you to know that tea is ready and that I'm cutting cake with my sword if you want some."

Oh, well that was a misunderstanding.

As I got to munching down some cake and sipping my tea, my thoughts drifted back to my own weapon. The Blade of End. Humanity's most powerful weapon, destroyed by Herobrine's Wither Skeleton. I still needed to replace it with something, but what could hope to match a weapon which had defeated both the Ender Dragon and Mr. Troll?

Rick noticed my discomfort and patted me on the back, "Chin up lad. We'll get you a new sword soon enough." I can only assume Steve told him what happened.

Here's hoping.

We spent the day recovering and figuring out our next move. Boris was completely out of it, but just to be safe Steve tied him up to the bed, making sure he couldn't attack us even if he wanted to.

"We need to rescue the others," I reminded Rick as we went over our plans for the seventh time.

He nodded, "Aye, but how do we do it? Red Robes is bound to keep them close to him now, seeing as we were able to rescue Boris. He's still got Amy, a cracking shot and Winston, one of the best fighters I've ever seen. There's no word from Viktor, though I'm certain they caught him too."

"We need more allies," Steve sighed, "but where are we going to get them? Overwatch is thousands of blocks away. Reinforcements wouldn't get here for two weeks at the minimum. Who can we expect to help us now?"

Rick paused, rising from sitting position and marching over to the window. Something told me what was going on in that big (though not as big as mine) brain of his.

"I think I have a candidate in mind for our mission," he said, "yes, he's perfect. One of the greatest soldiers and leaders I've ever known. If anyone can help us find Red Robes and rescue our friends, it's him."

"Been a while since we've seen the old chap," I chuckled, "I wonder how he's getting on."

"You don't mean…" Steve began.

"Oh I do," Rick nodded, "the old Commander of Overwatch."

A grin formed on my face, as the three of us stared out the window. Sitting in the distance on a small hill was the little cabin the former Commander had built on his hill. I wonder how he'd react to seeing us.

"WHY IN THE NAME OF NOTCH AM I TIED TO THIS BED?"

Day 6

Well, I suppose being the former Commander of one of the greatest cities in Minecraftia has its benefits.

The four of us were gathered outside his house, about to knock. We were all decked out in our combat gear, and Rick had even lent me his spare sword to use. I appreciated the gesture, but it didn't feel the same as my old sword.

"Is this really necessary?"

We still weren't 100% sure with Boris. Oh sure, we'd knocked his brain around with an Obsidian block, but we weren't entirely convinced he wasn't possessed anymore. What if it was all part of some trick to lull us into a false sense of security, before striking when we least expected it?

We couldn't take any chances, which is why we tied him up with several layers of string and removed anything from him that could be used as a weapon. Including most of his clothes.

"I'm freezing," he moaned.

"SILENCE TRAITOR!" Rick barked, "I mean, um, quiet you."

With that out of the way, Rick took a deep breath and knocked on the door.

"Hey Rick?"

"Yes Romero?"

"A thought has just occurred to me."

"Go on."

"It's kind of embarrassing."

"No worries, just say it."

"Alright then… do you know what the Commander's name is?"

"…"

"Your silence isn't reassuring."

"I never asked."

"You never asked?"

"Nope. I thought the others knew what it was."

"I don't know his name either."

"Oh for goodness sake Steve!"

"Can you blame me?"

"Well, this is going to be really embarrassing for-"

The door swung open.

"WHO DARES TO TRESPASS ON THE PROPERTY OF THE RETIRED COMMANDER MAXUS!?"

Talk about convenient.

The door flung open, and revealed to us the former Commander. The last I had saw of him, Maxus had been an imposing figure at two and a half blocks high, dressed in full armor and wielding a sword capable of cleaving a tree in two with one slice.

Seeing him in a pink apron was a little… underwhelming to say the least.

***

"And that's why we need you out of retirement," Captain Rick finished, "Herobrine has been delayed for the moment, but I fear he could return at any minute. We need your help to defeat his only remaining servant, a man we call Red Robes."

Maxus seemed to be thinking our words over, sipping from his tea and muttering to himself. Then, he walked over to the (still-chained Boris) and began fiddling with the locks.

"I don't think that's a good idea sir," I told him, but he just shrugged me off and finished removing the locks.

"Oh thank you," Boris beamed, "you have no idea how long I've wanted to- GACK!"

"Karate chops. So much more effective than chains," Maxus chuckled, "so you've come here to recruit me in your fight against Herobrine. I must say, I'm honored. Retirement is such a bore, sitting around all day and cooking delicious meals. Sleeping as long as you want and not having to worry about anything."

"Sounds pretty good to me," Steve chuckled, but Maxus ignored him.

"I've got my old weapons and armor in the back. I've been itching to use them since I got here, but the greatest threat I deal with is some zombie."

"Excuse me?" I spat out my drink.

"I don't despawn them," Maxus chuckled, "I just shove them into the ocean."

…

"I have only one more question…"

Maxus turned, that familiar fire burning in his eyes.

"When do we move out?"

Day 7
"I've sent word to Captain Jackson," said Rick.

Jackson. Once a member of Rick's personal squad, now his second-in-command. Apparently her beauty was only outshined by her skill with a sword. We zombies don't really see beauty. More often than not, we care on the number of brains one has consumed. Needless to say, I was very popular with the ladies.

"I thought you were a vegetarian," Rick noted.

…

Never mind.

"Jackson will assemble our army at Overwatch. Once we've dealt with Red Robes, we'll be launching an assault on the Nether."

"Is that wise?" Boris asked, "Herobrine has been dealt with."

"For now," Maxus stroked his beard, "but he could return. Commander Rick is making the right decision here. By attacking early, we can prevent any chance of Herobrine attacking with his forces."

"It wouldn't be an easy battle," I reminded the two Commanders.

"Of course not," Maxus chuckled, "but that's what makes it fun. We all enjoy a challenge."

Yes, I'm sure fighting the fiery forces of the Nether itself will make for a lovely weekend.

"It's not like we need to destroy his entire army," Rick noted, "all we need do is take control of Herobrine's Temple. His seat of power. Without that and with

Herobrine's capture, the remainder of his army will be scattered across the Nether.

Fair enough.

"So where's Red Robes?" I asked, "We can't fight him unless we find him. I trust you have a plan for tracking him down."

"There's no need," Rick shook his head, "I already know where he is."

"You do? Where?"

The Commander said nothing more, instead pointing into the distance.

***

Oldtown. Once one of the most powerful cities in the known world, now close to a ruin.

"What has he done?" Rick shook his head.

The entire city was flying banners, showing the, ahem, beautiful face of Red Robes. Many of the buildings have been destroyed or were currently burning. The citizens worked away in the streets, making pictures of Herobrine, coffee mugs of Herobrine, posters of Herobrine.

This guy was Herocrazy.

"What?" I asked the others, as they all ran from my incredible joke.

We soon arrived, once again, at The Museum of the

Fallen. A pair of skeletons guarded the entrance, but we quickly dispatched them and continued on our way.

"Just how powerful is this... Red Robes?" asked Maxus.

"Pretty tough," Steve admitted, "but Rick and Romero have defeated him twice."

"He seems to be getting tougher," Rick remarked, "last time he ended up sticking Herobrine's spirit inside my body."

"And I beat him when I had my sword," I reminded Steve, "I'm sorely lacking a Blade of End right now."

"YOU LOST THE BLADE OF END!?" Maxus bellowed, "DO YOU HAVE ANY IDEA HOW MUCH THAT COST TO MAKE!?"

"NOT A LOT, KNOWING HOW TIGHT YOU ARE WITH MONEY!"

"I'M GOOD AT YELLING TOO!"

"DO YOU KNOW WHAT TIME IT IS!?"

Oh dear.

Red Robes emerged from the shadows, dressed in his red pajamas and clutching a teddy bear, all while rubbing his eyes. Winston, Amy and Viktor followed behind him, dressed similarly. Upon seeing us however, they sprang into action.

"Well, this is turning into a lovely evening," Red Robes chuckled, "Boris, I see you've rejoined your friends."

"Not sure I'd call them that," he muttered, rubbing the spot where Maxus had struck him.

"No matter, I'll have you back with me soon enough. The question is how many hearts of damage I have to deal before you give in."

With the click of his fingers, our former companions sprang into action. Winston with his knives, Amy with her crossbow and Viktor with his hammer.

"How about we make things interesting?" Red Robes asked, "Right now, the odds are a little unfair. You outnumber my warriors by one, so I need to make up the numbers. Luckily, I have the perfect candidate in mind. More than perfect. You've brought in the old fossil, so I'll be bringing in someone from Rick's past as well."

Someone from Rick's past? Who could he mean? I glanced to Rick himself, who'd turned a very pale shade of white. The sound of footsteps echoed in the hall, and we were greeted with the sight of a fifth figure. He resembled a mummy, wrapped nearly entirely in bandages. The only thing that was visible was one red eye.

"Ladies and gentlemen, boys and girls, may I have the honor of presenting Rick's former partner in crime. Please put your hands together for Leon!"

Epilogue

"What news do you have?" Herobrine asked.

Before him stood three of the most powerful witches in Minecraft. One dressed in red, one in blue and one in a rainbow robe.

"Commander Rick has lain siege to The Cultist's fortress in Oldtown," the one in red spoke, "although we are not certain of the outcome, we believe that he will not emerge victorious."

"The Cultist has also managed to take control of several of Commander Rick's allies," added the one in blue, "The Marksman, The Brute and The Fighter all serve him. The Hitter has broken free of his control."

"Overwatch also appears to be preparing for battle," explained Rainbows, "Captain Jackson appears to be gathering the forces of the surrounding area, for whatever reason that might be. We can assume that Commander Rick has warned her of what is to come."

"Overwatch will barely slow us," Herobrine

chuckled, "once the gateway is opened, no army could hope to resist us."

"Be that as it may, Commander Rick's former squad is nothing to be scoffed at. We must be careful."

"Caution is not necessary," Herobrine waved his hand, "they shall join us or be destroyed. Now then, is there anything else to discuss before we begin the ritual?"

"One last thing," Rainbows spoke up, "Commander Rick has recruited Maxus, the former Commander of Overwatch."

Herobrine's face twitched.

"The same Commander who defeated you nearly fifty years ago."

"Maxus is old and weak," Herobrine spat, "last time he had Lady Luck on his side and I possessed but a fraction of my power. I'll destroy him like the rest."

That seemed to satisfy the three witches, who stepped up with their hands outstretched, each carrying a glowing crystal in their hands.

One red. One blue. One green.

Book 8: Herobrine's Return

Prologue

Jeez, as if things were not bad enough.

We had just managed to rescue Rick from the clutches of Herobrine, only to return home to find our allies had been turned against us. Faced with a difficult battle, we prepared for the conflict that would end all conflicts. An ancient battle to determine the fate of Minecraftia itself. A tale that would be remembered as the greatest war ever fo-

"Yo Romero! You want cookies with your tea?"

"I'm in the middle of something Rick!" I snarled

back, "But yes, I'll have some."

Ugh, that totally killed the moment. There I was, being all dramatic; ready to take on the forces of evil. Then Rick goes and kills it. Oh well.

Sup reader? How goes it? Chilling well I presume. Or maybe you're heating up. Hehe. Sorry, bad jokes are all I've got these days. You know, considering the world has gone and ended.

Oh right, you probably haven't reached that part yet. My bad.

Well in that case, let me be the first to welcome you to the end of the world. Don't hit yourself with the door on your way out. Better yet, don't let the countless hordes of zombies and skeletons get you either. Last thing we need is to pick your items up off the ground. Also, keep an eye out for the massive lakes of lava and the giant, one-eyed moon.

But how did we get here, I hear you asking. We last left off fighting against the Champions, right? Well, I suppose there's a few blanks to fill in. Sit back, wait for Rick to bring the tea and I'll tell you the story.

The story of how Minecraft came to an end.

Day 1

"Ladies and gentlemen, boys and girls, may I have the honor of presenting Rick's former partner in crime. Please put your hands together for Leon!"

Leon. Rick's partner. Supposedly despawned by none other than a sorcerer who attacked Oldtown years ago. As I watched this seemingly mummified figure stumble onto the battlefield, things started to click in my head. Pieces of the puzzle began to fit into place. Rick wasn't too far behind.

"It was you," Rick hissed, "you were the one who attacked all those years ago."

"Very good," Red Robes clapped sarcastically, "I did indeed attack Oldtown. I was going after the materials necessary to bring my master back. You two idiots were in my way and I had to dispose of you. Yet surprisingly, after I defeated your little friend, he still came after me. Followed me through the portal I created. We fought some more, where I struck him down again… I'll say this much Rick, he's a tough fighter."

You would have thought a reunion between friends would make for a happy occasion. But no, Rick, it won't be. Quite frankly, he looked ready to tear the room to pieces.

"I'll destroy you."

"Temper temper," Red Robes chuckled, "all Minecraftians obey me in the end. I possessed him, healed him and set him to work as my greatest servant. Watching from the shadows, waiting for the right moment to strike. You might have beaten my other cultists, but there's no way you'll trump Leon."

"We defeated you easy enough," I reminded Red Robes, "and we've got more than enough manpower on our side to take you down."

"Or so you think," Red Robes sighed, "I should probably warn you that Leon is much stronger than anything you've faced. Heck, I'd bet on him winning if he fought you guys solo. Still, we'll keep this fight fair. And once you've been defeated, we can all settle down and celebrate the return of my great master. ALL HAIL HEROBRINE!"

"That won't be happening," Steve grinned.

For the first time, Red Robes hesitated. He tilted his head towards Steve, raising an eyebrow beneath his hood.

"What do you mean?" he asked.

"Herobrine's been defeated," announced Rick,

pointing his blade at Red Robes, "he no longer has a host and he's missing one of his precious power gems. He's trapped in the Nether as a spirit, never to be released again. Oh, and the only remaining portal has been destroyed. He's gone for good, Red Robes. Your master won't save you this time."

"WHAT DID YOU DO!?"

Flames erupted around Red Robes, splitting the floor into several sections. Lava poured from the cracks, and the pillars supporting the ceiling threatened to topple. Even our possessed friends looked a little nervous.

"FOOLS! HEROBRINE WOULD HAVE MADE THIS WORLD A BETTER PLACE! BUT YOU JUST HAD TO INTERFERE, DIDN'T YOU!? SO BE IT! IF HEROBRINE CAN'T HAVE MINECRAFT, THEN I'LL MAKE SURE NO ONE CAN!"

One moment, Red Robes was floating on the other side of the room. The next, he appeared in front of Rick. A click of the mouse later, and the Commander was sent flying. Steve rushed to the robed figure, but the latter merely ducked under his sword swing and knocked him to the floor.

"DESTROY THEM!"

Winston, Amy and Victor charged towards us, brandishing their knives, crossbow and hammer respectively. Leon wasn't far behind, floating through the air instead of walking. Lazy guy. Red Robes set his sights on me, but his burning red eyes failed to catch sight of Rick launching a counter attack, namely a blast of lightning from his swords.

"Here's the plan," said Rick, "I'll handle Red Robes. Boris, use your speed to counter Victor. Steve, take down Winston. Maxus, same goes for Amy. Romero, I'll trust you to handle Leon. Don't hurt him too much; just knock the mind control out of him."

"Roger that," I nodded, twirling my sword. Sure Red Robes had bragged about this guy's power, but how tough could this mummy actually be?

"Heroes, attack!"

And so the battle began.

It was nothing short of impressive. Every moment was utterly breathtaking, as Minecraft's greatest warriors battled to their very last heart. Truly a spectacle players would pay money to see.

I remember Rick taking on Red Robes, both the Sorcerer and his lifelong enemy, one on one. How Red Robes called upon all sorts of powerful spells, from fireballs hot enough to melt stone to skeletons as big as a house. I remember how Rick dealt with each of these threats in turn, before launching a ferocious counterattack and bathing his opponent in lightning.

I remember Steve against Winston. Now that was something spectacular. Steve, a master of the blade, against the champion of knives. They moved too fast for the eyes to follow, the clinging of their weapons creating a sort of music. The deadliest dance of them all. Yet as Winston attempted to catch his peer off guard by pulling a hidden knife, Steve merely knocked it aside and threw his enemy to the floor.

I remember Maxus battling Amy. I'd seen the former Commander fight in the past. Ferocity and skill, all coupled into a body filled with wisdom. Amy must have fired twenty bolts at the elder warrior, but Maxus dodged each and every attack, before moving in close and dashing her crossbow across the room. She tried drawing her backup sword, but that too was knocked aside. A second later, she had surrendered.

I remember Boris and Victor, two rivals duking it out. There was not a force on earth that could match Victor's strength. The guy was built like diamond. Yet for all that muscle, he was just too slow to catch Boris in his stinking leather armor. The hammer was built for up-close and personal encounters, whereas Boris could just step back and bonk Victor over the head, again and again, until the giant gave in.

And then there was Leon. The wild card in our little battle. Still, we'd beaten everyone else. There was no way I'd let them down.

Or so I thought.

I started things off nice and simple. A slash towards my foe's chest. Easy enough to dodge, which I was hoping Leon would do. I'd then follow up with an elbow to the chest, hopefully knocking him down and bringing this fight to a swift end.

However, as I swung my sword, Leon ascended into the air. The bandaged man floated way out of reach, and before I could figure out how to respond, I felt a great force strike me. A powerful gust of air, conjured from nothing, tossing me around as if I weighed no more than a grain of sand.

"You will fall," Leon declared, throwing me into the ground. So he knew a few tricks. No matter, I had some of my own

"Distortion Wave!" I shouted back, slashing the air front of me. A wave of energy was released, flying towards Leon. He called up a shield, as I guessed he would, causing the attack to explode against it. The bandaged man was covered in cackling blue electricity. Right now, he would not be able to see anything. Now was my chance.

Slipping behind his floating figure, I conjured up another one of my tricks. Zombie Breath. No human could resist the urge to fall asleep after catching a whiff of this. With a chuckle, I breathed it into the air, aiming to envelope my opponent in the stench...

And yet, somehow, in some inexplicable way, he dodged it. He vanished from his spot in the air. A popping sound rang out behind me, and as I turned, I was knocked back once again. Battered aside, this time too weak to get up.

"Stay down," he cautioned, as he rounded on the others.

"LOOK OUT!" I yelled, spying Amy's crossbow a few blocks away. If I could reach it, maybe I could turn this situation around.

Steve and Boris moved in first, aiming to attack from the left and right. Leon was not having that though. He deflected both motions, and followed it up with a ceiling-shattering blast of air. Another two down. Maxus tried a different approach, feigning a strike to the right before pulling out a bow and firing. But even that failed to work, and he too was defeated.

That left only Rick against his former friend.

"Leon, it's me..." Rick muttered, his sword falling from his hands, "Me! Your old friend Rick. Your partner. We used to be bounty hunters, remember?"

I had finally reached the crossbow. It was a high-tech weapon, capable of capturing an enemy, all the way up to despawning them. I set it to stun and loaded a fallen bolt.

"For the love of Notch, please remember," Rick begged, "I don't want to fight you."

Leon paused, dropping back down to the ground. He scratched his head thoughtfully.

"Rick?" he muttered.

ZAP!

"Gotcha!" I grinned, as Leon fell to the floor, unconscious, "Another victory for the good guys."

"Seems that way, doesn't it?" Rick asked, examining the now sleeping Leon (kinda like sleeping lion, hehe).

"Ow, my head," I heard the voice of Winston moan as he rose to his feet. Amy and Victor shortly joined him. Red Robes also tried getting up, until Steve and Maxus pinned him to the floor.

"All over for you I'm afraid," Maxus shook his head, "Herobrine's beaten and your little mummy didn't stand a chance against us."

"NOOOOO!" he yelled, in typical villain fashion, as I walked over to him.

"Now then, let's see who's really behind that hood!" I announced, pulling back the article of clothing.

"GASP!"

It was…

It was…

Some guy with a really bad haircut who we'd never met before.

"Do we know this guy?"

"Doesn't look familiar."

"I say we shave him."

"DON'T YOU DARE!" Red Hair spat, "THIS IS THE FINEST HAIRCUT IN MINECRAFTIA!"

"Cut it all off," ordered Commander Rick, much to our delight.

"NO, WAIT! WAIT! I BEG OF YOU! DON'T DO THIS! NOOOOOO!"

Ah, all's well that ends well right? No more Red Robes, no more mind control and certainly no more…

BOOM!

Herobrine…

Day 2

"Rick, pass the biscuits would you?"

"Sure thing Winston."

As if things weren't bad enough. Herobrine rules the world once more and we are out of custard creams. Oh how I hate this stupid, blocky world.

Okay, you're probably looking for an explanation. Well I've got good news! There isn't one. We've got no idea how Herobrine managed to acquire a new body and escape the Nether. We were a bit distracted by fireballs raining down on our heads and the thousands of zombies rising up from the dirt blocks. In seconds, villages were pulled into the ground and entire cities crumbled.

There is good news of course. Overwatch is still standing, thankfully. Rick's old squad managed to assemble its army and seal up the city, protecting everyone inside. Last we heard, they're being besieged by millions of zombies. I wish them luck.

As for us, you needn't worry. We're currently holed

up in Maxus' house on the hill.

"You do realize this place was only meant for me," he muttered, walking into the room while wearing a pink apron.

"Yes yes, now make with the food! We're starving!"

"Yes sir."

Thankfully, the undead have never been smart. Well, other undead have never been smart. My IQs so high they haven't got a number to measure it. But for my poor brethren, climbing up a hill is very difficult for them. Maxus removed all the stairs and so far, only three of them have made it up. The rest have fallen to their demise.

"Well, we've got a working farm," I heard Rick talking strategy with Winston and Steve, "we could easily hold up here. For the next few weeks, months, or even years. But we're not here to hide. Right now, we need a plan to find and take down Herobrine."

"And how do we do that?" asked Steve, "Our last encounter didn't go all that well."

Ah yes. Racing outside, only to find Herobrine hovering in the air in all his glory. It was probably the shortest fight I've ever been a part of. We had our butts kicked in 2.3 seconds.

"FEAR ME!" Herobrine demanded.

"NEVER!" Rick shouted back.

"Oh come on, please?"

"Master, you have returned!" Red Robes skipped outside, "Oh how happy I am to see -"

"SILENCE MORTAL!" Herobrine floated back down to earth and grabbed Red Robes by the... well, robes, "You can start by making a fresh pot of coffee! Then, you can run down to the bank and deposit all your money into my vault. Once you're done, you can..."

With the unholy lord of darkness preoccupied, we decided to leave him alone and visit another day. We managed to make it to Maxus' house at the same time the entire planet exploded...

That's bad, right?

"Very," Maxus nodded.

"Bad!" Victor cried into his hands.

Well, aside from Herobrine now ruling over the world and us running out of biscuits, there is a third problem we need to deal with.

"So when are we going to let Leon out of the basement?" I asked.

"When he starts behaving," Amy replied, "he bit me last time we tried to get him out of there."

I sighed. Rick's old friend was proving to be quite the nuisance to us. Red Robes had placed a powerful spell on him, because no matter what we tried, he was unwilling to cooperate. He attacked us whenever we grew close, and only grew angry if we tried to lock him up.

"A bucket of milk might do the trick," I pointed out, "that stuff can erase any magical enchantment. Question is where are we going to find it? Herobrine decreed that all cows be kept protected from the evil humans."

I glanced at Boris, who looked very comfortable in his leather armor.

"We can worry about getting Leon back later," Rick sighed, "right now, we should probably focus on dealing with Herobrine."

"And how do we do that?" Winston questioned, obviously annoyed, "He defeated all of us in the blink of an eye. None of our skills can even come close to damaging him, especially now that he is at full power."

"The Blade of End would have done it," I noted, "but Herobrine seems to have thought ahead. He got rid of that weapon before making his full return."

"We seem to be forgetting something here," Rick pointed out, "Commander Maxus, you defeated Herobrine about fifty years ago. How did you manage it?"

"With a lot of luck," he chuckled, "Herobrine had found the secret exit to the Nether. I was searching for the bathroom at the time, and managed to catch him as he entered the real world."

"Even my jokes aren't that bad," I shook my head,

as the room groaned.

"Oh fine. This old-timer just wanted to have a bit of a laugh. Defeating Herobrine... it went something like this."

And so, we entered the flashback.

Fifty or so years ago, the soldiers of Overwatch received terrible news. A village to the north was under attack from creatures which hadn't been seen in centuries. Zombie pigmen, both vicious and tasty at the same time. I was a Captain at the time, and the Commander of that era immediately set out with our army to the village.

When we got there, we found the villagers had been transformed into undead creatures. We managed to restrain them and return them to their normal forms, but by the time we were finished, the zombie pigmen had returned. Thus began a brutal battle to save the village from these invaders.

It was a long fight. Many of our soldiers were despawned, and there seemed to be no end to the creatures. We soon discovered the source of their reinforcements: a Nether portal at the center of the village. As my comrades kept the enemy at bay, I managed to stab a diamond pickaxe into the Obsidian, cutting the connection off from the Nether.

We dealt with the stragglers and gathered our remaining forces at the town square. It was at that moment we heard a terrible scream come from the library, shortly before it exploded into a thousand pieces. When the smoke

cleared, Herobrine himself was hovering above the crater.
The destroyer of worlds. The one who had battled Notch to
the end in the god wars.

We readied our weapons for a fight, but something
seemed... strange. Herobrine didn't look to be at 100%.
Far from it. He was panting heavily, his clothes were torn
and he was struggling to stay afloat. For whatever reason,
he didn't as much power as he normally would. Still, he
called upon those blasted fireballs of his and began his
attack.

Despite being weakened, he put up quite the fight.
Another three were injured and two more were despawned.
We were getting desperate. That's when I spotted it. A
glowing artefact around his neck. A necklace. I couldn't
believe I hadn't spotted it before. It was so obvious! A
necklace, glowing bright red. Heck, it was almost blinding,
that's how bright it was.

Still, if my years in the Overwatch army had taught
me anything, it was that glowy stuff was meant to be
targeted. With that in mind, I rushed Herobrine as his
attention was distracted and cut the object off. It fell to the
ground and immediately ceased glowing. The white-eyed
figure stared at me for a few seconds, his fists clenched,
before fading away into nothing...

Back to the realm of reality.

"I've been thinking about that day a lot," Maxus
told us, "and I've been trying to figure out just what that
necklace did. It was as if it was draining Herobrine's

power, forcing him to fight us on even terms. Our top scientists couldn't figure it out, so we just left it in the vault."

"Maybe Herobrine needed it to stay in the real world?" I suggested, "You didn't destroy a physical body, meaning he still hadn't regained his old one. That meant the only anchor he had to this world was that necklace. Maybe it took a lot of his power to juice it up?"

"You could be right," Maxus nodded, "yes, I believe so. That attack was probably to get Herobrine a more permanent body. Still, what on earth was he doing in that village's library?"

"The village north of Overwatch..." Rick muttered, "Crofter's Village?"

"That's the place. What about it?"

"They have a vault, similar to the one used in Overwatch," Rick pointed out, "Do you think they could have something important there?"

"Might be worth finding out," Maxus nodded, "though I doubt all of us need to go there. I say we split the group in two. Half of us can head over to Overwatch to help free the city from the attackers, while the other half makes way for Crofter's Village."

"Alright then," Rick agreed, "Maxus, feel like taking up your old position?"

"Retirement was getting boring anyway," he

chuckled, "I'll take the champions with me, along with Leon. The magicians there should be able to help him out."

"Sounds good," Rick nodded, "so Steve, Romero and I will head over to this village. If we can find what Herobrine was looking for before he does, maybe we can figure out his ultimate plan."

"Aside from destroying the world?" I groaned, "Great. More stuff to deal with. Not that I had plans this weekend."

"Suck it up Romero," Steve chuckled, "by the end of this, we'll be the most popular people in Minecraft for saving the world so many times."

"Point taken. Alright then, let's do this!"

Here we go again. Off to save the world one last time...

Day 3

Today was the day.

Our two groups stood just outside of Maxus' house. Rick, Steve and I stood on one side of the garden, while Maxus, the champions and a restrained Leon was on the other side.

"This is it then," Maxus began, and we nodded.

"The final FINAL battle," Rick chuckled, "at least until the next bad guy comes along. But what's the chance of that happening?"

"Pretty high I'm afraid," Maxus shrugged, before laughing himself. Soon, we were all joining in on the merriment. Even Leon was giggling from beneath his bandages.

"I'll make sure Overwatch is still standing by the time you get back. Do what you have to if it means defeating Herobrine, but don't take too long. The rest of the world doesn't have a lot of time."

"Well, it was certainly nice to see you again

Maxus," I waltzed over to him and shook his hand, "here's hoping we get to meet up for a meal when this is over."

"I can never tell if you're being sarcastic," Maxus sighed, "no matter. Anyways Romero, I need something from you."

"I'm not paying for the food you made us," I protested, "quite frankly, you're a terrible cook."

"Then I guess I'll never bake you cookies again…"

"I BEG OF YOU, PLEASE FORGIVE ME!"

"Alright, that's enough," he pushed me off his leg after I'd grabbed onto him, "What I was going to ask for was that sword hilt of yours. You still have it, right?"

"What? Oh yeah, sure," I tossed him the hilt of the Blade of End, not entirely sure why he was asking for it.

Then he showed me a pair of Obsidian blocks floating in his hand.

"But… how? That stuff is the rarest material around!"

"Then you should open your eyes a little more and use that crafty brain of yours," Maxus shook his head, "you do realize you were carrying a block of the stuff this whole time? I only found it while washing your clothes."

He was right! From the cells! The one they had

made us sleep on. Hah. Joke's on Red Robes.

"Hang on a minute," Rick interrupted, "where'd the second piece come from?"

"You can thank yours truly for that," Maxus gave us a thumbs-up, "While you lot were busy fighting Herobrine, I snuck back into the museum in Oldtown and stole this from the portal. You're welcome, by the way."

"And how does a sword hilt and a few rare blocks help us out?" Steve demanded.

"We can reforge the Blade of End you fool."

I could tell Maxus was probably looking for an excuse to slap him. I spared the old commander the trouble and hit Steve myself.

"Hey!"

"You really think you manage it?" I questioned him.

Could it even be forged a second time? This was no ordinary weapon. This was the very sword that had stopped the Ender Dragon and defeated Mr. Troll. An object of untold power, that could be the only hope of stopping Herobrine if all else failed. Could they really replicate such a feat?

"Of course it can be forged a second time," Maxus looked at me as if I was an idiot, "this is Minecraft fool! Repairing is as easy as a few mouse clicks."

"Mouse clicks?"

"I said nothing."

"But…"

"NOTHING!"

***

Crofter's Village.

There was not much to say about it. A few wooden buildings might have been here before, but right now, the entire place was filled to bursting with zombie pigmen, seeking out their next victim. The fact that we had managed to get here was a miracle in its own, considering the state the world was in.

"Many, who would have thought Herobrine would have set traps for people wandering the landscape?"

"Of course he would have! But those traps are only for idiots."

"Hey, don't blame me! I'm really hungry."

"Gah, whatever. I'm just saying that I didn't expect a pile of pork chops in the middle of nowhere to be so deadly."

We got bombarded by Ghasts the second Steve tried to grab the food. Still, all dangers aside, we'd finally made it here. Said to be the location of Herobrine's most sacred treasure… well, not really. I had to make something up to keep the journey entertaining.

"So where exactly are we headed?" Steve asked, as he cut down the five-hundredth zombie pigman of that day.

"The library," Rick replied, "the place Herobrine went last time. Hopefully, we'll reach this artefact before he does."

"And there's nothing to suggest Herobrine's already found it?" I checked with Rick, who shook his head.

"I don't think so. This village is close to Overwatch, so it was fairly safe for a while. The soldiers might have been defeated, but they still bought us some time. Let's just hope it was enough."

Rounding one of the corners, we came across the library. A very sorry looking structure, with half the roof caved in and a decently sized group of pigmen awaiting us.

"FOR OVERWATCH!"

"FOR THE CHAMPIONS!"

"FOR ZOMBIE KIND!" I cried, following my companions into the fray.

The fight was short, sweet and netted us tons of those glowing XP orbs. Totally worth the five minutes of our time it took to complete.

"Can we hurry this up?" Steve asked, pointing to a growing horde of pigmen behind us.

"Think you can buy us a few minutes?" I asked my companion, to which he nodded.

"Get moving," he told us, "find whatever's hidden here. I'll make sure these guys won't give you any trouble."

"Good man," Rick declared, patting him on the back.

"Let's go," I pointed to the back of the library, shoving a few bookcases down to block the path behind us.

"Over here!" Rick called out to me, pointing to a crack in the ground. I highly doubt anyone would have missed this before. This was fresh.

"You don't think..." my thoughts turned to Herobrine growing even more powerful than he already was.

"We better move!"

As we climbed down into the darkness, I heard the screams of my ally a short distance away.

"NO! GET BACK! GET BACK! NOT THE ARM! ANYTHING BUT THAT! I USE IT FOR BACK SCRATCHING!"

"He was a good man," Rick sighed, "ah well. I'm sure he'll respawn soon enough."

"He'll be pretty sore," I grinned.

With those comments said, we finalized out descent

into the chamber below. With only a spare torch to light the way, Rick examined the surroundings of the room. It was composed of mossy cobblestone, the likes of which you would only find in the oldest of dungeons.

"This place is pretty ancient," I said aloud, "but what's it for?"

"I guess we'll soon find out," Rick pointed ahead. There was a tunnel leading to parts unknown, and there was already a torch lit over there. Our weapons readied, we proceeded to the light source.

"Maxus said Herobrine pretty much tore this place apart looking for something... what do you think it was?"

"I couldn't tell you if I wanted to Romero. Whatever it was, it was worth Herobrine risking his life to do last time. If we can beat him to it, then we might just have a chance at defeating him."

"Must be a pretty powerful object..." I remarked, but I immediately shut up as we reached the end of the hallway. We were here.

And so was Herobrine. His back turned to us as he was bent over, working on something. Rick raised a finger to his lips, as he passed me the torch and grasped his blade with both hands. With careful footsteps that sounded no louder than the falling of a feather, he approached his foe.

There was no way it would be this easy... would it? Could Rick end it with one lucky blow? Was Herobrine too distracted to see his demise sneaking up behind him?

The answer of course, is no.

Rick swung his blade, a blow which would have despawned Herobrine immediately… if it had actually been him. The apparition disappeared in a poof of smoke, and the real Herobrine dropped down from the ceiling, forcing the Commander to the floor.

"Rick!" I cried, unsheathing a dagger and preparing to throw it. I met some resistance however, when someone roughly grabbed me from behind and yanked on my arm.

"Not so fast," the rough voice of Red Robes gasped, as he shoved me forward into the room.

And just like that, we'd been defeated.

"So this is the best Minecraftia has to offer?" Herobrine sneered, "The same two heroes, time and time again. Aren't they getting bored? They could really do with a fresh new face."

"I do agree master," Red Robes nodded.

"SILENCE FOOL!"

"Why don't you tell us what you were looking for down here?" Rick demanded, "Must have been important if you got your butt kicked by Maxus."

"Such bravado," Herobrine chuckled, "but it's worthless. You've been well and truly beaten this time. I saved my best trick for last."

"Say what?"

"You thought I'd come down here looking for something… shows how much you know."

Herobrine stepped aside, revealing just what it was that illusion had been working on. A gemstone, much bigger than the ones we'd encountered before.

"Last time I was in Minecraft, it wasn't to look for something. I wasn't going to waste time with that. No, I came back to hide something, in the one place no one would ever look."

"You mean a village beside the most secure city in Minecraft?" I raised an eyebrow.

…

"SILENCE!"

I felt my lips shut themselves.

"I stored the most powerful of all my weapons here, planning on using it when I made my return to Minecraft."

Showing us his gauntlet, currently powered by three gems of red, blue and green, he revealed a fourth slot on the back of the wrist.

"I control the world, but only in the present. In the past, I was defeated. In the future, I might not exist. Well no longer! Using the fourth gem I concealed on Minecraft, I plan to travel to all timelines. I shall visit each era of Minecraftia, and make my power known! Not even Notch will be able to stop me. If I am defeated once, I shall only rise up again, even stronger!"

"Like that'll happen," I threatened, having finally had enough of Herobrine, "you'll never stop us. We'll find a way to stop you Herobrine. That's a promise."

"Ah, but you won't," Herobrine wagged his finger, "for you see, there's one visit I'm making before I take control of time itself. One visit that'll make sure you never, ever interfere with my plans again."

"Tell me Romero, what was it that caused you and Rick to meet?"

"A battle in the swamp," I opened my mouth without thinking.

"Exactly," Herobrine grinned like a maniac, "and what if you two were to never meet? What if you never became close friends? What if the Ender Dragon was never stopped? What if Mr. Troll caused all sorts of chaos? What if you two were never there for Minecraftia?"

"Don't do it," I pleaded. I genuinely pleaded. I couldn't allow this to happen.

"I'm begging you Herobrine! Don't do this!"

A life without Rick? Without Steve? Without Maxus? Without the champions? No…

"Too late I'm afraid," Herobrine sighed, "best say your goodbyes now, for this time Minecraft is finished!"

And with that, he was gone.

And then the room began to melt away, as if time itself was being undone…

TO BE CONTINUED

Made in the USA
Las Vegas, NV
12 December 2021

37306252R00177